Child of Dreams

Dream War Saga, Vol. 1

Credits
Publisher: ManChild, Ltd.
Author: David Thompson
Editors: Alexis Ross, Michael Thompson
Cover Art & Design: Matthew Pelzel, David Thompson
Interior Design & Layout: David Thompson

Based on the EverLore Campaign Setting, and the Boundless Gaming System, developed by David Thompson. Special thanks to Amy, David, and Caleb Thompson for always believing in me, to Matthew Pelzel for his work on the cover design, and to my parents for giving me the strength to never give up. *"I miss you both."*

ManChild, Ltd
670 Northland Blvd., Box 18237
Cincinnati, OH 45240
www.ManChildLtd.com

Table of Contents

Map of Midian

A Continent of Mythandria

NOTE: Most of this novel's action takes place in, and around, the region known as the Archstone Range. This area is home to a collection of cities and villages that do not have a centralized ruler, but which maintains strong alliances to safeguard against attacks from outside forces.

Prologue

The air was thick with heat and moisture, making the waiting soldiers uneasy. They had marched hard for the last two tendays, never knowing why, too afraid to question the pale one. It had been a hard march. The weather had been unusually harsh for this time of the year. Spring was usually a time of much rain and gentle breezes. But there had been no rain, no tender breezes to cool their scorched bodies. The sun had been their only companion; from dawn to dusk, it was there, glaring disapprovingly at the army below. For half a month, the soldiers had tolerated this glare with much agitation, but today, it was not the same. The sun seemed to abandon them, leaving behind angry heat, as if to say that it would have nothing to do with what was soon to come.

"The men grow anxious," whispered Zendrick as he bent low in the saddle. Even as he did this, his eyes darted about, looking at the faces of the men of his army. He looked all around the rim of the small valley, only to see a solid line of soldiers, *"his soldiers,"* he tried to remind himself. His long thin face seemed even more misshapen as sweat rolled from under his stringy, dark brown, hair.

"The time is soon," whispered the pale figure standing beside him, who scarcely lifted his eyes to regard the obviously nervous Zendrick. "You'll have this day, my lord," the figure, known to him as Solas continued with as much feigned respect as he could muster. "Look," he said as he raised his arm and gestured down the hill. Beside him, Zendrick winced as the speaker's hand slipped from underneath his too long robe, and the pale and decaying flesh on it seemed to crawl under the intense inspection of the weak light of the day.

Wrenching his eyes from those hands, Zendrick hazarded a quick glance at the man's face. It was a face that once may have appeared perfectly normal. But now seemed possessed of that placid hue reserved solely for the dead and was void of any semblance of emotion. The man's eyes were pallid green orbs adrift in sunken sockets. His pale skin was rubbery and cold, which gave the impression that his flesh was merely a garment; taught, and exact, but not skin.

"My lord," words familiar, yet strangely foreign to him, jarred Zendrick from his search. Before him sat three silver clad warriors, two humans and one vlel, on dark horses. Each warrior had a hand resting calmly on the hilt of a finely crafted sword.

"My lord Balenwald has considered your demand, and found it lacking," responded the brown-skinned vlel in the middle of the group. His voice was stern and forceful as he addressed Zendrick. "He will not give unto you the possession of his wife and unborn child. Furthermore, he orders you off of his land," and with that, all three riders turned their horses and rode calmly towards the heavily walled village of Silverwood.

"This valley shall be yours," whispered the pale figure, excited by the prospect of bloodshed.

"The time is now," shouted Zendrick, as he looked to his right and nodded to a trumpeter who was waiting patiently by his side. The trumpeter eagerly began the call to war. The whole valley grew eerily still as a stiff breeze began to blow. Sensing the soldier's hesitation and excitement, the pale figure beside Zendrick stepped in front of his lord's horse and began chanting a psalm of ancient days. As if a spark had been struck amidst a bale of hay, the chant was taken up by the soldiers around him and within moments could be heard all around the valley. *"Hail the Dark Lord. Hail his fallen Knight. Hail the stolen power that gives us our might!"* Then came the attack.

The village of Silverwood seemed easily over matched, as three thousand heavily armed warriors rapidly descended on the village that housed less than nine hundred able bodied soldiers. Even as a volley of arrows was released from archers on the wall, killing with each arrow released, the oncoming soldiers seemed not to notice. A madness appeared to have gripped them as they stepped over the bodies of their fallen comrades. They cared not; their only goal was the destruction of Silverwood.

Ladders forced upon the wall could not be pushed off fast enough, for as one would be toppled, three more were there to replace it. The soldiers of Silverwood worked feverishly to keep the enemy from breaching the walls. Running here and there, they slashed at any man or woman close to the top. Yet, it was to no avail. There were too many ladders to be repelled, too many warriors to be killed. All seemed lost as the lord of Silverwood looked down from his perch, his sword dripped heavily with blood. He could see that his men would soon tire, and the enemy would be upon them.

"Begin the dream cast," shouted the lord from atop the wall as he slashed at yet another invader, catching her in the neck causing her lifeless body to smash heavily onto other soldiers trying to climb the same ladder. In the village, a green clad mage stepped out from a small hut near the center of the village. Her tightly curled hair rose in a bush around her beautiful face as she squared her lean shoulders and walked forth with a confidence she did not fully feel. Looking around, the mage could see the desperate situation the village was in. From the warriors on the wall to the villagers in the street, the mage felt a surge of hopelessness.

Not having time to escape the coming onslaught, the women and children were placed in a large building deep in the village. As the mage walked past, she looked at the faces of the people who stood in the doorway. She searched the crowd, until at last she found her quarry.

Lady Balenwald stood amid a host of frightened women, each trying unsuccessfully to hide their growing fears. Her eyes were afire with determination as she pointedly caressed her swollen belly. No words were spoken as she and the mage locked gazes. The elderly mage stared at her for a moment more, drawing strength in her presence, for Lady Balenwald was dearly loved and respected among the villagers.

Reluctantly, the mage turned her attention to the battle and the soldiers that even now threatened to overrun the village. In deep concentration, she opened her mind to the Shadow Sea and caressed the flow of magic as she began to envision runes of power that had been passed down for generations; the call of the dream-cast. The air around the mage began to hum as the magic of the spell grew within her. Cheers and shouts of joy began to rise from the village soldiers on the wall as the spell began to take effect.

On the ladders, the invading soldiers began to scream in pure agony. Many hurled themselves off the ladder to escape some unseen horror while others hung tightly to the ladder shouting incoherently, each trapped in a personal world of torment. Looking up at their comrades, the invaders started slowly backing away as they too began to feel the effects of the dream-cast. Shouts of fear and pain began to sound up and down the line as the magic went to work in full force. A large circle opened as one of the soldiers, shouting about maggots in his skin, began to run his dagger gleefully across his arm. Even as he opened huge gashes in his arms and the blood began to flow, he kept on, until he was tackled by three of his fellow soldiers who in return begin to squirm on the ground agonizing over repeated snake bites.

From atop of the hill, Zendrick watched in fear as his army started to fall apart. He knew that the magic that had gripped them was a magic as old as the Great Wars, and feared that he too, would soon succumb to its perverse images.

"I told you this would happen," he spat at the pale figure beside him, "they have the magic of the mind's eye. We cannot hope to win in this engagement."

"Win, my lord," smirked the pale man, "we shall not only win, we shall annihilate the putrid citizens of this dismal valley, or have you so soon forgotten the gem which our patron has given you?" he continued. Gesturing at the bloodstone pendant around Zendrick's neck, the pale one whispered in a slyly devious voice, "Use the power."

A smile spread across Zendrick's face as he grabbed the pendant and excitedly fingered the bloodstone like some mischievous child. The depths of the gem seemed to draw Zendrick into itself as he concentrated on the magic within. Anger and hatred erupted from Zendrick as he lost his fear and reached out towards the mage beyond the walls.

Within the village, deep in concentration of her own, the old mage suddenly jerked back and fell to her knees. Blood dripped from her nose and seemed to drain from her brown skin as she forced herself once more to her feet. Understanding that she was facing a power well beyond her ken, she stumbled over to where Lady Balenwald stood. The mage knew she could gain strength from the obbin'nor "the power of the gods" that resided within the unborn child. Once there, the mage reached out her hand, then hesitated, not sure how to proceed. Understanding the intentions of the mage, Lady Balenwald took her hand, and pressed it firmly against her stomach. The mage felt a rush of power run through her veins, filling her with the strength to complete another powerful spell that sent Zendrick flying off his horse.

"Power, power," stammered Zendrick as a line of blood began to run down the length of his face, "She has too much power, I cannot defeat her," he finished as he rested against the hind leg of his horse.

"Allow me to help, my lord," whispered the pale figure with obvious contempt. Anger filled the pale figure as he thought of how weak this human was. Lord, Zendrick was not worthy of such a title, but still, the pale figure could not be totally disappointed for he could feel that the village mage was not working on her own. He could feel the work of the ancient magic here, and although Zendrick was in possession of a very powerful pendant, he lacked the strength needed in himself to actuate the truest of the gem's abilities.

Stepping forward, the pale figure pulled his robes tight to his body as if drawing power against the light of the day. With his head lowered, the pale one began to levitate into the air, for he wanted all to see his might. He looked down on the soldiers below him. Those who were not in the throes of the mage's spell, looked up and pointed him out to those around them. For the warriors on the wall, the dark image that now appeared in the sky sent an ominous signal that the day was not yet won. Fear rippled throughout the ranks as their eyes settled on the pale figure hovering over them like a black void.

Opening wide his arms, the pale figure tensed as he released a ripple of magic that could be visibly seen to all. The defenders of Silverwood followed the ripple as it moved over their heads, and into the village to slam with bone-crushing force into their mage, who went crashing through the walls of a nearby building. Weak convulsions wracked the mage's ruined body for a short period before she lay still in death.

"Destroy this village," commanded the figure in a voice that resonated in the minds of all who were there, "but touch not the mother whom we seek," he finished, and with that he slowly descended to stand beside the shaking Zendrick.

"The village is yours," he whispered to Zendrick as he watched the soldiers attack with renewed vigor.

Burning arrows were sent over the village walls into the streets below. The warriors fought hard to defend their village and their Lord, but to no avail. The invaders breached Silverwood's walls in several different places and poured in like an angry tidal wave. Within two hours, the village lay in ruins.

Once he was satisfied that all was secured, Zendrick went into the village were bodies lay haphazardly amidst the scorched structures. He smiled as he contemplated his victory and smiled greater still as two of his generals approached escorting Lady Balenwald between them.

"Your impatience has gained you nothing," Lady Balenwald spat as she stared defiantly into his eyes. "My child, which you so desire, has still another fourteen moons before her time on this world. And I shall see myself starved to death before I let you have her."

"My dear lady," Zendrick began, as a dark smile

washed over his face, "it will not come to that, for I have other means of extracting my prize." Even as he spoke, a man approached carrying an old leather satchel, from which he produced several wicked looking knives.

"Oh, I'm sorry," said Zendrick, "Have you not met Vellubus, he used to be the tending physician for one Vizithian or another, before he was forced out. I believe that it was some fuss about perversion in his work. But now he is all mine." he concluded as he turned to address Vellubus who was staring at his newest victim. "Extract the child, then see that the alter is prepared," ordered Zendrick as the last of the fires in the village was dowsed. "Do it quickly, for I desire to be away from this wretched place as soon as possible." With that, he retired to the large tent that had been constructed for him a short distance outside of the sacked village.

Once inside, Zendrick fell heavily into the fur covered chair resting in the middle of the tent. His mind raced with excitement, for not only had he succeeded in destroying the fabled village, but before the end of the day, Zendrick would make a sacrifice to Madrigonus, his shadow born benefactor. This would be no ordinary sacrifice. Indeed not, Zendrick would sacrifice the Silver Child, the Child of Dreams, the daughter of Pantos Balenwald, the elven heir to the great obbin'nor power of Omoarnus Balenwald, the original ruler of Silverwood.

"You have your sacrifice," hissed a voice, seemingly from nowhere. "You have the wielder of the old power. She who would become the Child of Dreams. She who is descended from that once mighty nation known as the High Born. She who caries within her the blessings of Danu, the misguided Goddess of Nature. Tonight, the child shall perish, and with her shall end the hope of all of Midian."

A gleam drifted into Zendrick's eyes as he relished every tainted word spoken by the pale figure that materialized before him. He grew excited every time he was told of this sacrifice, because with it came the promise of great power. This specific ritual would transfer the power within the child into the wearer of the bloodstone pendant that now rested on his chest. Zendrick closed his eyes and allowed himself to bask in the belief that he would soon possess such a great force.

"You will be leaving us then," questioned Zendrick, knowing the answer as he spoke the words.

"I go to prepare a place for you in Demarnia," the robed figure responded.

"Demarnia," said Zendrick, sitting stiff in his seat, "That island is a wasteland," he continued, "Not since the time of the last mongrel uprising has anything lived there. If we go to Demarnia, it will mean nothing but death for me and my army.

"Ah, but you forget," replied the figure, as he raised his hand to calm Zendrick. "You forget that Demarnia is the land of Madrigonus, claimed for her by her once great champion, Nimrotha. Surely our wise patron would not see her new champion die on the eve of his greatest triumph," the speaker dropped his head to mask the smile on his lips, for he could see how Zendrick's eyes came alive at the notion that he was Madrigonus' new champion. "Even now, I am in the process of restoring a great walled city long believed destroyed. It was the abode of Nimrotha and now shall be yours."

Seeing that his words had had their desired effect, Solas bowed low and slowly faded into darkness and was gone. His passing left Zendrick alone in silence. It was an odd sensation, Zendrick noted, for he had not had much time to himself in quite a while. Relaxed and at ease, Zendrick's mind drifted to that fateful night in the temple of Bakarri (Goddess of Darkness).

Zendrick had been praying to the goddess, laying bear the pain of his broken dreams, when the pale figure appeared out of the shadows. He shifted uneasily in his chair as he relived the fear at the pale one's coming.

"Fear not, Lord Zendrick," whispered the figure in a deeply melodious voice. "Your destiny is one of greatness," the pale one continued as he produced a shiny ruby from within the folds of his robe. With a mere gesture, the figure sent the ruby floating through the air to rest inches above the still frightened Zendrick.

"Wh-whhh-whho are you..." Zendrick stammered. He glanced up at the pale figure noticing not only the white ashen skin, but the sunken eyes and decaying flesh. "What are you?" he asked, gaining a modicum of composure.

"My name is Solas," answered the figure as his robes parted revealing the disturbing flesh within. "I am, or was, a darkling; one of the lost children of Fa'al, the Candle Maker. It is for you that I have come, for I have heard from Bakarri, The Underworlder. It is her desire that you wield this gem," he finished, gesturing to the ruby.

"For what purpose?" questioned Zendrick.

"To lead her army in the war to come," answered the figure as he turned to leave.

"Wait," called Zendrick, causing Solas to turn, "Where are you going, and what do I do with this?" Zendrick finished as he grabbed the floating ruby. At its touch, he felt a gentle tingle slowly extending from his fingers to his arm, then through the rest of his body.

"That is your gift," spoke Solas as he noted the curious expression that washed over Zendrick, "and where I go, is where I go." With this, the figure bowed low and disappeared.

The weeks following that meeting were ablur with action, excitement, and exhaustion. Each day, Solas would instruct Zendrick on the use of the ruby's magic. They would wake early in the morning, and work late into the night. In six months, Zendrick had become quite efficient with the ruby. It was around that time that Solas convinced Zendrick to test his new might by engaging in bloody combat with all comers, be they seasoned warrior or confident mages. Before long, Zendrick was picking fights in taverns, inns, alleys or main roads in every village he entered. As promised, the gem's power held true. And with every victory, word of his glory spread.

Through the whispers of Solas, Zendrick found his way to an old fortress that housed a ragtag group of miscreant warriors that made their living from causing harm to others. It did not take long for Zendrick to bend these weak men to his will. But that of course, was only the beginning. The power of the ruby attracted people from all over. The fortress soon became a magnet for those disenchanted with their current station in life. Pit fighters, murderers, rapists, and the like were all accepted into Zendrick's growing embrace.

Nearly four years from the day of their initial meeting when Solas told him of the Child of Dreams, Zendrick felt more assured of his power. Still, the thought of adding the ancient magics to his growing abilities intrigued him and thus he determined that he must carry out this sacrifice as swiftly as possible.

"It is time, my lord," stated a young warrior, drawing Zendrick back from his contemplations "The altar is built and already the sun is setting. The sacrifice must be made now, if it is to be done this day," added the woman as she bowed low in apology for her interruption.

"I am ready," replied Zendrick as he followed the warrior out of the tent. There was a feeling of excitement in the air as the soldiers, that had come to witness the sacrifice, opened a hole for Zendrick to pass through. The altar was situated near the center of the village, so only a portion of Zendrick's army could actually attend, the rest, were busy setting campfires, enjoying the spoils of war, or getting drunk in the name of celebration.

Upon his approach, a man clothed in orange, walked up to Zendrick and bowed low in respect. He then offered up to Zendrick a dagger of pure obsidian. Zendrick admired the dark blade with growing anticipation as he accepted it with trembling hands. He quickly walked towards the altar where another orange-robed man waited, holding a bundle in his hands. As he grew closer, Zendrick could see that inside the bundle was the child wrapped in blood-stained cloth. Zendrick's hand tensed around the dagger as he stood beside the altar.

"The sacrifice is prepared, my lord," stated the orange-robed man as he voiced the words of an ancient magical rite, causing green ethereal runes to blaze into the evening sky. He then placed the baby on the altar, and sprinkled drops of blood on her head. Stepping forth, Zendrick lifted his dagger high. Taking one last look at the helpless child,

Zendrick shouted in the most powerful voice he could muster.

"This death, in this place, of this holy child, for our unholy reason, is for the glory of our Lady Bakarri. Let it serve as a sign of our devotion. Thus, dies this child." With these words, Zendrick plunged the dagger directly toward the baby who lay blissfully unaware of the death speeding in her direction.

A green streak sped through the air smashing into Zendrick's descending wrist, sending the dagger flying awkwardly away. A shout of pain escaped Zendrick's lips as he pulled back his arm to see an arrow sticking through his wrist. Confusion and panic swept through the attending warriors and priests as one arrow after another sped into their unholy ranks.

A deep growl sounded immediately in front of Zendrick, who fell back as a massive dark-furred hound materialized out of thin air, mere inches from the warlord's face. Zendrick, fearing that his life was forfeit called upon the ruby and projected a solid wall of force between him and the advancing threat. But to his surprise, the beast paid him scant attention. Instead, it hurtled for the alter and scooped up the bundle in its massive jaws. Before leaping at the readying crowd of warriors. Yet even as its mighty paws touched soil, another growl erupted from within the warriors as a second hound barreled in, delivering death with savage delight, clearing a path for the first hound's retreat.

"Stop them at once!" Zendrick shouted angrily.

Recovering from the initial shock, some warriors took off in pursuit while others searched the area until they spied the previously unseen attacker who continued her deadly stream of arrows. She stood alone, between two large oak trees, a mace hanging easily on her firm hips. Her tightly braided hair, piercing black eyes, and beauteous brown face belied the deadly gleam in her eyes. Her expression was one of death as she continued her deadly barrage of missiles.

Seeing only one woman, no matter how deadly, the warriors took heart, and drawing their weapons, charged her. As if welcoming the challenge, the woman dropped her long bow and gracefully pulled out her mace. As the first of the men cleared the trees, the woman bent low and leveled the mace with devastating force into the warrior's ribs, sending him staggering back into his fellows. Her next move came swiftly as she stepped towards the rush of men, swinging her mace in an upward arc lifting yet another warrior off his feet.

The next four warriors stepping between the trees were equally ill prepared as a blue clad swordsman stepped out to meet their advance. The warrior sank his sword deep into the belly of the closest man and without a moment's pause, reversed his momentum, retracting his sword and twirled in a leftward arc. This time, his blade sliced across the neck of the next man in line. Even before the lifeless bodies of the two men hit the ground, he stepped passed them and lifted his sword to deflect the third soldier's blade, while at the same time using his left hand to release a sparkling dagger that hammered the fourth soldier in the chest. Stepping forward, he shot a whimsical wink at the third warrior before adjusting the angle of his blade and sending the screaming warrior to face Yen-Lo, the terrifying Judge of Souls.

"We have what we came for Borack," shouted the woman as she turned and darted away from the warriors. As she ran, she produced a small vial, which she hurled at a nearby tree. When the vial burst, its contents spilled out on the tree. Instantly, the liquid began to dissolve the tree and the very air around it.

She watched as the two hounds sped past her and dove into the shimmering portal created by the released magic. Borack was next and playfully griping, "Winchunset, why must you always spoil my fun?" as he too disappeared into the portal. Winchunset's full lips parted into a smile, as she turned and bashed her mace into the face of one of the men who had gotten too close.

Then she too, stepped into the portal, and was gone.

Chapter 1:
The First Dream

"What is it girl?" whispered Z'har as he approached the huge chaga hound, whose thick mane of brown and tan fur blended easily with the surrounding foliage. "What do you see?" he continued as he peered into the darkness below, letting his eyes adjust to the waning light. The horse sized canine made no sign, but lowered her shoulders closer to the ground and bunched her powerful muscles as if she were an arrow ready to be loosed from a bow.

From his vantage on the cliff, Z'har could see much of the vast expanse of the Palen Wood, nestled within the shelter of the Valley of Shale. So far, the area below was empty, but Z'har trusted the senses of Zion, one of the two chaga hounds bound to him since the time of his youth. If she indicated danger approached, then it was so. The gray elf ran a hand along his bald head before slipping his sword free of its scabbard and prepared himself for the signal from Niska and Bodica, that would draw him into combat.

As he waited, Z'har's mind flicked back through the years to the very first time he saw the valley. He must have been around eight years of age, when Borack Fallow and his wife, Winchunset, decided to stop running and make their home on the "mountain" known as Isla'nuwar in the dense woods within this mysterious valley. The term mountain is often used lovingly to describe the place, which the dwarves who know a thing about mountains, understand to be more of a rather expansive hill. While not the largest peak within the valley, Isla'nuwar does reach well above the tree line and is cherished by the dwarves who maintained the fortified enclave known as Skyfall, within and around its solid core. At first, the dwarves were hesitant to have Borack staying within the zone of protection offered by Skyfall, but Azoria Casillas, an old friend of Borack and a respected member of the community, convinced the elders to provide shelter for Borack and his would-be charges.

Even at that age, Borack was a hard task master and pushed Z'har (and others of his "children") hard in their training. Long arduous years, and short often-sleepless nights followed, as he and the dwarven residents of Skyfall taught them to fight, track and hunt. It was a long process that became more intense when Winchunset and Belitar Botryogen started instructing them in the ways of spellcasting.

Looking back, he could almost hear the frustration in Winchunset's voice as she soon realized that Z'har would never be a powerful mage. Perhaps it was his zin nature, that caused his mind to drift amid the tumultuous flow of the Shadow Sea, the plane from whence all magic flows. Regardless, Winchunset soon came to realize that his unique essence provided the benefit of shielding Z'har from most magical attacks. Thus, his training focused more on how to neutralize mages, rather than casting harmful spells. Though Z'har did not understand it at the time, his zin abilities had saved him many times over his eighty-three years of life.

Z'har remembered those training sessions when Winchunset would conjure some magical foe for him to battle. At first the sessions were harmless because the opponents were simple illusions. However, over the years, particularly once Borack and Winchunset started bringing other children to their grove the training became more dangerous. Winchunset began summoning lesser devils and demons for the growing number of youths to face in combat. When he was around seventeen, Borack and Winchunset started taking him, and a select few of the Fallowsheir, as the children would come to call themselves, out on raids into the nearby forested areas to keep it clear of the intrusion of the mongrel races. But all of that changed thirteen years ago, when Borack and Winchunset simply vanished. Now Z'har, the eldest of the seventeen Fallowsheirs, patrolled their home territory much as his adopted parents had.

A low growl brought Z'har out of his reverie, as Zion crouched low and began to descend through the dense forest. Before following her, Z'har caught the faintest glimpse of movement through the trees below and knew that Niska and Bodica were on the move. Catching up to her, Z'har rested his left hand on Zion's muscular shoulders, mentally urging her to restrain her furry. He knew she had no love for the goblins and orcs that lived within this valley but understood that they did not want to attack before the trap was set. Sensing Z'har's concern, Zion ran her rough tongue over his arm and relaxed her ears as they took up position in an outcropping of boulders that jutted out of the forest line.

Looking out, Z'har could see the first of the mongrels that had wondered into his territory. It was a goblin with exceptionally long ears and overlarge teeth. The creature cast about with its beady eyes before motioning for its companions to follow. Z'har counted eighteen goblins but was a bit surprised when two gnolls stepped out behind the goblins. One of the gnolls said something in their guttural Mud Tongue, but Z'har was too far away to make it out. In response, one of the goblins peeled off from the rest and hurried to bring a small chest to the waiting gnoll. Taking the chest, the gnoll gave the groveling goblin a swift kick to the shins and motioned for him to kneel so the gnoll could sit on its back. The other gnoll gathered close as another thirteen more goblins marched out of the forest to rest with their fellows. The goblins didn't seem particularly interested in the work of the gnolls and busied themselves by digging into their packs and pulling out various bits of meat and bread to munch on, or by examining their bandages, which were evidence that they had seen combat recently.

The seated gnoll, opened the chest and pulled out a parchment, before handing the chest to the standing gnoll, who placed it gently on the ground. The two gnolls then began to inspect the parchment that was now unfolded into a much larger piece. Z'har was unable to hear their conversation, but from their gesticulations, assumed that the parchment contained something that was very important to them.

Z'har did not have much time to contemplate the scene before him since the head of the standing gnoll exploded as a vine-like metal missile burst through it, interrupting whatever he was saying. Even as the stunned goblins and gnoll began to react, a furious wolvn burvore stepped out of the tree line and lifted her hand, before pulling it down as a closed fist. In response to her actions, the ground beneath four of the nearest goblins erupted with chains of earth and rock, wrapped around their necks, and then savagely dragging them into the earth's embrace.

The sitting gnoll stood up, and snarling, extended his hand as if to respond with a spell, only to have his growl of anger turn into a welp of pain as a massive set of jaws clamped down, severing his arm at the elbow. The terror in his eyes was nearly palpable as a massive chaga hound with black fur, shot through with burnt umber stripes, materialized around those powerful jaws. Standing fully six feet at the shoulders, Bodica swiped a heavy paw across the gnolls face, dropping him in a shower of blood and broken teeth.

"Alive," shouted Niska, as the wolverine-like humanoid stepped to the fallen gnoll and quickly inspected his broken body. "Well, it looks like he'll live long enough for us to deal with this bunch," she finished as she pulled out a sword that looked like aged bark and stalked towards the confused goblins.

Bodica released a howl of rage as he vaulted over the kneeling goblin and slammed into a group of seven goblins that had managed to get their weapons out and form up into something of a line. The line might have lasted more than a few breaths, had a slightly smaller chaga hound not materialized behind the goblins and waded in, drenching her brown and tan fur in the blood of the dying.

"So much for a signal," shouted Z'har as he darted from his place of concealment directly into the path of three fleeing goblins. Quick as death and final as thought, Z'har's blade cleaved through the advancing leg of the nearest goblin, before finding a home in the throat of one of her companions. Without looking his left arm came up to block the axe chop from the third goblin. However, the strength of that blow was not expected, and Z'har found himself turned to the left by the force of the blow. Instinct took over as Z'har rolled with the momentum and launched into a sideways spiral that saw his blade cleave the head of the goblin in a right to left swipe, before completing his twist and landing smoothly on the ground.

Even as Z'har's blade rammed through the spine of another goblin, he saw Niska duck low under the swipe of a goblin before vaulting into the air and grabbing the goblins head in her powerful claws. The goblin whined as the momentum of Niska's jump carried her past that goblin, leaving long bloody scars as she came down feet first on the next goblin in line. Riding her target to the ground, Niska's free hand was a blur as she stabbed the creature to death.

"Stay present," she yelled to Z'har with a slight look of concern on her face. Yet, seeing the young elf wending a path of death through several more goblins, she knew that her fears were misplaced on this day. Z'har's dark gray skin caught the last embers of the dying sun and his focused eyes, that darted to her with a quick wink, let her know that he was still him and that this battle would soon be over.

Confident in the abilities of her allies, Niska calmly picked herself up and walked over to the unconscious gnoll with a missing arm. Reaching out to the Shadow Sea, she shaped the flow of magic into the desired current and laid her hands upon the bleeding creature. As the effects of her Death's Door spell swept over the gnoll, she watched as his wounds closed while leaving him oblivious.

"So, where was that signal you mentioned?" asked Z'har in a half serious manner. The elf had fought beside the burvore long enough to know that, even in her haste, she would never do anything to put him, or his two chaga hounds in danger.

Grabbing the limp gnoll by the shredded remains of his armor, Niska dragged him over and dropped him at

Z'har's feet. The look in her eyes was one of fury tinged with more than a little sorrow. "You must have been too far away to hear their conversation. Amid talking about covering their "allotted territory" they mentioned slaughtering a shakaran family just a league or two from here. The thought of this mangy mob killing the Skatterclaws, who had been so kind to us all these years, was too much. Their blood called to be spilled, and I was only too willing to answer."

With that, she spat upon the gnoll, before stating, "Just do what you do, and be quick about it. By my estimation, there's still one to many of these creatures left alive. I mean to rectify that as soon as possible."

Knowing that Niska was not one to speak of death lightly, and battling his own growing rage over the death of the nearby family, Z'har kneeled by the slumbering gnoll and slipped his fingers around the creature's skull. Centering himself, Z'har felt that familiar tingle that traveled from the base of his spine up to his skull, which finally raced through his hands to draw him and the gnoll into the plane of dreams.

Chaos swirled within the mind of the gnoll as dark spectral creatures seemed to stalk him from the depths of the creature's own despair. Scrambling on his hands and knees, the gnoll sought in vain to find a respite from the death streaking towards him. Suddenly, giant grey hands seemed to materialize out of the very miasma around him, grasping the gnoll in a vice-like grip before yanking him roughly into a land of dreams and nightmares.

Tumbling uncontrollably through a swirl of thought and memories, the gnoll caught a glimpse of a gray elf falling alongside him. The elf did not seem to be enjoying this any more than the gnoll did and expressed his displeasure by bearing fangs that seemed larger than the mouth that surrounded them. However, the gnoll did not have time to contemplate this development as he found himself standing on a battlefield about to launch a devastating spell at a fool hardy burvore, when his arm simply disappeared in the mouth of a savage nightmare hound dripping with the blood of a thousand foes.

The gnoll did not feel the pain of that contact, but the fear was enough to send him jumping back in dread, only to land on plush pillows of a forest home. The gnoll watched in satisfaction as his goblin underlings ransacked the home. His attention was drawn from the looting to the screams of the female shakaran, the homes rightful occupant, as she watched her male companion be flayed in front of their three worthless children. The gnoll, licked his lips and stood from the stolen pillows, walking over to the helpless female and grasping for a dagger at his belt. He would enjoy this. The screams she would make, the terror in her heart, the light of hope draining from her eyes…

The rough hand that grasped his shoulder, eliciting a cry of pain, as the wicked gray elf whirled him away from that wondrous scene, and uttered a growl of pure fury. "Not here, not what we are looking for. Show me why you here in my woods." The dizziness returned as the ground seemed to fall away below them and vision after vision sped by in a cacophony of sound and sights. Ordinarily, the gnoll would have laughed at how ridiculous the gray elf sounded with his rough use of the Mud Tongue, but the pain of that hand on his shoulder was all encompassing, and only relented, when at last their jumbled trek ended in a scene that played out several months prior.

The hindgar gnoll stood with others of the Knife Gut clan. Ten great warriors of his people, basking in the glory of their adoring clan and the gathered throngs of goblins and even orcs. All fell silent as a massively muscular female mastin gnoll strolled onto the dais within their makeshift camp. Standing fully nine feet tall, Gurktrog was the undisputed ruler of the clan. In her hands she held a stack of parchments, which she handed to each of the assembled ten. Her voice resounded like the thunder as she shouted, "We will find the temple, and through that we will find immortality!" A great cheer erupted from the tongues of the masses like lava from a too long dormant volcano.

Raising her arms to the sun, she pulled down a golden crescent of star and this too did she divide amongst the ten. "When you locate our destiny, speak into this, that we may know your location and come to claim our prize. Take sixty warriors each, scour this gods-forsaken valley, and do not return until your task is done." The gnoll filled with honor upon receiving the golden disc. Reality shifted ever so slightly and the gnoll found himself watching with savage glee as his war party broke off from the clan and began their hunt.

"Ooh, ha, ha, ha, owww" yelped the gnoll for his laughter over the coming events turned to pain even as his body transformed into a large shadowy figure walking down a long hallway of a well-appointed home. Z'har experienced a dizzying sense of confusion as the picture came into focus and his eyes followed a thin steel chain that trailed from the figure's right hand to the shackled hands of a small humanoid child. Z'har's thoughts were muddled as the figure stalked past him without any hint that his presence was noticed.

The same could not be said of the child, for truly she was a child. Z'har could see that now and his heart broke as he gazed at the tiny vlel girl with light brown skin, long braided black hair, and light gray eyes that pierced his soul with the suddenness of thought. Z'har guessed that the half-elf child was in her early teens, as she stopped and stared directly at him.

"Are you here to rescue me?" asked the little girl with hope shining in her eyes like the noon day sun. "I didn't think anyone would hear me. I have been crying for help for so long, but this place is so scary and makes me weak. Please, please hurry. I don't feel right. I think this place is making me sick."

"Uh," Z'har found himself at a loss for words. While Z'har had gained the ability to dream walk nearly thirteen years ago, his mastery of the process was severely lacking. Typically, he could only coax fragments of memories from others, only able to communicate with someone's dreaming mind through touch. But this, having someone totally alien to his eyes communicate so openly with him, was a new experience all together. "I'm sorry young one, but I don't know what is going on or how you are even here. Who are you?" he managed after settling into this new reality.

"I am Leloni," stated the child as the scene shifted to a large audience hall that found her sitting on a small pillow several paces behind and to the right of the shadowy figure that sat in a large ornate chair and addressed a throng of wraith-like supplicants. Z'har watched through vertigo-ladened eyes as the shadowy figure raise his arm and yank at the chain, soliciting a small cry of pain from the child. Even as the sitting child responded to the demands of the shadowy figure, a spectral aspect of Leloni appeared in front of Z'har and ran to him and wrapped him in an embrace birthed of desperation. "Please hurry, you have to come help me. Weldar is so cruel."

Z'har returned the child's hug and opened his mouth to form a response, when his mind was blasted by an agonizing force that had him drowning amid an onslaught of jumbled memories that had come too fast for him to comprehend. When Z'har's senses returned he could see that Leloni had been ripped from his arms and was being held aloft, by a gray skinned figure who ran the child through with a sword of pure glass. A torrent of torment escaped the child's lips as the assassin tossed her body roughly to the ground and turned to meet Z'har. "It will ever end thus," said the figure. Z'har froze with shock and a tinge of horror as he took in the image of the assassin… it was like looking in a mirror for the image that stood before him was the very image of Z'har. "We cannot escape our destiny," the copy continued as he took a step towards Z'har, who could only watch in utter bewilderment as he approached, …himself?

"No," whispered Leloni as blood trickled from her sad lips. She struggled to lift her head off the ground to gaze at the stunned Z'har and mouthed, "Help." With that single word, lightning struck and sundered Z'har's connection with the Dream Plane.

"I have what we were seeking," whispered Z'har as he tried to stand, but proved too weak to do so. He sat in exhaustion and horrified confusion. Who was that child? Why had he seen her? And why had he killed her? Emotions roiled within him like the pounding of sea waves that threatened to sweep him under their dark tide. Sensing his distress, Bodica came up and rubbed a wet tongue across Z'har's cheek. "Gross," shouted Z'har as he took a half-hearted swipe at the big hound and resigned to complete this mission before contemplating what the Dream Plane had showed him. "You know you can only get away with that because I haven't mastered this new ability yet. But watch out, because when I do, I'm going to take you on a jaunt through the Dream Plane," he finished with a weary laugh.

Silent as death, Niska stepped passed Z'har and emptied her canteen on the slumbering gnoll. Sputtering awake, the gnoll instantly read the situation and his screams soon filled the surrounding forest as Niska sated her rage at the atrocities the warband had committed. Only after she was finished, and the gnoll had breathed his last, did Niska turn to Z'har and ask if he was okay.

"I'll be fine. You know that takes a lot out of me. But this time it was different. There was someone else in there with me. A child. I don't know how, but I felt as if she was pulling me in. I mean, she was asking for help or something and I wanted to aid her, but in the end…" Z'har trailed off, as an image of his blade sinking into the child's flesh gave him pause. What did that mean, he thought before answering Niska's unspoken words by saying, "In the end, I think it is more than I can understand. What I do know is this whole region of the valley seems to be in danger, and Skyfall must be notified at once."

Those words seemed to have the desired effect, as Niska, ever the pragmatist switched focus from him to gathering what information she could from their foes before preparing to head back home. Z'har knew that Niska was aware of how shaken the dream walk had left him, but as usual, she would let him open up when he was ready. She was always better at reading people than he was, and once again he wondered to himself why she seemed to gravitate towards him more than any other Fallowsheir. Regardless, it didn't really matter, he was just happy of her friendship as he followed Niska, Zion and Bodica back to the west and the peak of Isla'nuwar.

Three days later, the sun was riding high in the sky of the late-fall early-winter morning as Niska and Z'har left the edge of the broadleaf forest. Before them stretched a patch of land nearly twenty acres wide and half that long, which was home to a small farm. This one was used for planting corn and potatoes, if Z'har's memory was correct. Even now, he could see the farmer in the distance, surveying the land with two children in tow. No doubt, he was passing on knowledge of the family trade to his heirs. Upon seeing them, the man gave a short wave of acknowledgement before returning to his task. Z'har noted several figures in the trees not far from the farmer and his family. From this distance, he could not make out their faces, but from their clothing and bearing knew they were members of the Sky Guard.

Niska waved back and stretched the weariness out of her shoulders as she took a drink from her canteen. "It's good to be back," she said, passing the canteen to Z'har who took a heavy swig.

"Too true," he replied as they once again pressed forward. Even though they had reached the outer edge of Skyfall territory, they still had several hours of travel left. As they passed by several other fields and pastures, Z'har caught a glimpse of one of the nine mounds, large, fortified, stone and metal domes, that were used for food storage and place of refuge in times of trouble. Each mound had a single entrance that faced towards Isla'nuwar that was guarded by warriors of many different races. The mounds had tunnels that connected them to an unterland garrison through which aid could swiftly be deployed.

After nearly an hour of walking, Niska darted ahead into the massive outgrowth of needleleaf trees that surrounded Mt. Isla'nuwar. After a moment, Z'har could hear the surprised shout of Untog, as Niska had ferreted out his watching post, and playfully sprinkled water on him from her canteen. Soon thereafter, the big, blonde-haired human came ambling out of the dense trees, with Niska astride his shoulders. "We win again," Niska said as she launched herself off her friend's shoulders. Untog's strong shoulders barely shifted as the burvore sailed into the air, but his smile grew even larger as he saw a familiar shimmer appear a step behind Z'har.

"I think you spoke too soon, little one," purred Kittlite as the jaguan shakaran gently placed her blade to Z'har's exposed neck. "At best, I'd say this one is a draw. Wouldn't you agree dear brother?" she continued as she placed a gentle kiss on Z'har's cheek.

"I would say that I was expecting that," Z'har countered, "but the truth is you're getting better. I didn't sense you at all. At least, not until it was too late." Tussling the thick tan fur that covered Kittlite's head, Z'har could see the faint traces of residual magic dripping from the dark rosette patterns that dotted her coat. "Of course, you do know that we still would have won. You two are good, but Niska's skills are great, and me, well… I'm me." Z'har finished with a wink and a smile.

"Whatever, short stuff," said Untog as he scooped Z'har up into a huge embrace. "We were starting to get worried about you two. All the other groups have returned, and the news isn't good. How are the pups?" Untog stated as he released Z'har.

"The hounds are fine. I sent them away to get some rest as I suspect their might will be needed if we are to weather the coming storm," answered Z'har as his tone became more solemn. "I fear our news will only serve to make matters more tense. Enough talk, did Ghost Hound station you here, or were you out on your own?"

"The Ghost has us here, and has our other siblings spread out across Skyfall," Answered Kittlite, as she too assumed a more serious tone. "Whatever it is that you guys uncovered, has the whole community on edge. We'll expect to hear all about it when we see you later."

"Until tonight then," said Niska as she clasped her sister's forearm and gave her a gentle squeeze.

Two hours later, Niska and Z'har sat outside Skyfall's primary audience chamber, known as the Eagle's Spire. The thick stone doors to the audience hall were open, allowing Z'har to see the mighty carvings of warriors representing prime specimens from each of the four dwarven subgroups (soaren, shield, mayrin, and volkn) standing as guard over this entrance and the opposite one that opened to the magnificent balcony, from which much of the valley could be viewed. Within, Eagle's Spire was a large, round, domed room with intricate carvings of enchanted glyphs scribed on the walls. At its center rested a heavy stone table in the shape of a hexagon, with seating enough for eighteen people. Nine wondrous pillars stretched from the floor to the ceiling, representing the nine races of the Prime (the first sentient beings of Mythandria, and the only ones known to have been created by Bushima, The Allfather).

The afternoon sun streaked through the balcony opening and glistened on the silver wings of Brassore Calamine, the youngest of the three current rulers of Skyfall. Just then, Brassore turned his head to acknowledge Niska and Z'har, calling them forth with a wave. Intense black eyes gazed out from a handsome, thickly bearded, bronze face as Brassore put aside the papers he was studying and gave the two his full attention.

"I assume you have been briefed on the news provided by the other scouts. It seems that things are about to become a bit livelier in our little sleepy part of the valley. I understand that you two had an altercation with a band of raiders. Tell me your tale."

Seeing that Mihoko Nurak, the second ruler of Skyfall, as well as an assembly of senior members from Skyfall's War Cabinet were in attendance, Z'har took the lead as he was the eldest of the Fallowsheirs their de facto spokesperson in matters of politics. As he recapped the experience of their mission, Niska presented Brassore with the map, and several missives they recovered from their fallen foes, before taking a seat by Z'har's side. The letters were written in a combination of Mud and Mage Tongue. While Z'har was fluent in Dwarf Tongue, Elf Tongue, Wood Tongue, Oromo and Prime Tongue, his mastery of other languages was sorely lacking. Luckily, Niska had full understanding of nine languages, and was able to read the messages and relay their importance to Z'har.

His recitation of the events faltered a bit as he debated how much to reveal of his strange experience while dream walking. However, he knew that some of the individuals in this room were much more versed in the ways of magic and mysticism than he and figured they might be able to provide answers to the questions that still plagued him. He also explained that every night, since the encounter, he had dreams of the child and her death. While relaying this part, Z'har was careful not to let his eyes drift to Niska as he had not shared this detail with her and could already feel her concerned gaze on him.

When Z'har was done, the room was silent for a short while as Brassore passed the collected items around for the others to see. When all present had inspected the items, Pyrophane (the youngest member in attendance, and also a Fallowsheir) stretched out his hands and opened his third eye. All three of his eyes began to glow causing the table's interior to appear to dissolve into sand. From the sand rose a detailed replica of the Northwestern region of the Valley of Shale, where Skyfall was located. Even as Pyrophane started speaking, Z'har could see tiny sand particles coalescing into walking figures.

"Well, this confirms it," said Pyrophane as a massive congregation of creatures materialized further to the south and east of Skyfall. "The Knife Gut clan is definitely up to something, Gurktrog has sent out at least eight war parties that we know of." Here, eight groups of figures broke off from the larger mass and spread out in many directions. Two of them entered areas within several day's journey of Skyfall. "Our reports indicate that the Knife Guts are more than seven thousand strong. If they decide to turn their full might on our region, we will be hard pressed to repel them, certainly many of the outer communities not directly under our banner would be lost."

"Is this a thing you have seen, Pyrophane, or a simple strategic assessment?" asked Mihoko Nurak her blue eyes alight with their usual intensity.

"This assessment is not a result of a vision," answered Pyrophane, referring to one of his innate zin abilities to catch glimpses of the future. "It is as you say, a product of my understanding of matters martial."

"Regardless, I agree with your assessment," stated Mihoko as she turned to address the others at the table. "I feel this is just the beginning of something greater. As I have already expressed to some of you, I feel there is distant current within the Shadow Sea that threatens to become a typhoon if not properly addressed. Perhaps, the actions of Gurktrog's minions are but the first salvo, in a much larger conflict to come."

"If your words prove true, then we must tighten our defenses, and prepare to assist the other communities in the region," responded Brassore, for truly his thoughts had been running along the same lines. "It is Olorun's wish that we be ever ready to fulfill the duties for which dwarves were made. The protection of others is a duty that is most sacred. How best do you think we should proceed?" This question was posed to the room at large.

Over the course of the next few hours, plans were made on how to provide aid for the surrounding communities, as well as to sure up Skyfall's own defenses. Radelerz Dekalbite, a powerfully built shield dwarf, and First Commander of the Sky Guard, indicated that a hand of soaren dwarves (five individuals) should be sent to the five largest settlements in the area to notify them of the danger and offer refuge to any that would come to Skyfall. This was readily agreed upon, but Brassore stated that two hands should be sent so that the aerial messengers would travel in pairs. Other plans were made, with input from all.

After many hours, several of the attendees left the chamber to begin implementing the various plans that had been discussed. Z'har and Niska were about to make their leave, when Mihoko raised her hands and bid them to stay. "I thank you for the information you provided and for how helpful the Fallowsheirs have been in guaranteeing the protection of Skyfall, but this news of the dream has me vexed." She turned to Pyrophane, as Z'har and Niska resumed their seats. "Pyrophane, tell them about the vision you shared with me two days ago. I believe this might have some bearing on the dream walking experience of Z'har"

Pyrophane gave Mihoko a respectful nod, before addressing the chamber. "I was in the Rainbow Meadow when a vision came to me. In it, I saw Niska and Z'har in deadly battle against dark creatures. They were aided in their struggle by warriors that are foreign to my eyes. At one point, I saw Z'har wrapping a small child in a protective embrace, but in the very next second, he plunged a sword into her heart. Following that, all faded to black, until Niska appeared, riding Zion with a noticeably wounded Z'har strapped across Bodica's back." As he concluded, Pyrophane sat in silence allowing everyone to digest his words.

He then turned to Z'har and Niska before continuing. "As you know, my visions are not prophecy set in stone, but only probabilities of likely outcomes. Mihoko and I were at a loss as to the vision's meaning, but now that you have experienced your own encounter with this vlel child, I believe fate is pulling your strings away from Skyfall. And even though I cannot say for certain, I think this may have something to do with the disappearance of our parents and why we were gathered in the first place. I know we do not speak of this often, but their absence is still missed all these years later and the mystery surrounding their vanishing has never truly been explored," this he said casting a sideways glance at Mihoko who had made several unsuccessful attempts to locate their adopted parents in the past, "nor explained."

Sensing the unease in Niska and Z'har's eyes, Mihoko added, "This does not mean that you will be away from Skyfall forever, but I do think there is something here that must be ferreted out. Maybe it is the fact that you and the child share the same elven heritage, even if she is only half elf, that has given you knowledge of her. I know this is just a guess, but the laws of magic do not always cooperate when it comes to zin. I will perform some castings tonight and consult with others to see if we can come up with some guidance as to where the child can be found. If we can discern that, then I am sure we can procure a map for you."

The elder dwarf's voice softened as she leaned more fully on the table and addressed Niska and Z'har with something akin to sorrow in her eyes, "I know that we have discussed the uniqueness of your zin nature, but you must not underestimate the hatred that some mages have for your kind. Even though zins are extremely rare, they are often viewed as an abomination, as your innate abilities seem to belie the foundations of the great flow of magic that is the Shadow Sea. Some, perhaps even most, mages feel that zin are a scourge to be hunted and destroyed."

Here, Mihoko opened her hand, and an illusory image of a glyph strewn ring materialized and hovered over her palm. "The rings I created that are even now fused to your spine, will mask your essence from all but the most powerful mages. Your passive abilities will mostly go unnoticed, but you must use your active talents with care, lest you give yourself away in the presence of one that would seek you harm. Know that it is not just mages that you must concern yourselves with. Often, they have the ear of wealthy lords or ladies whose ample resources can be turned into a weapon against you."

"And here at last," sounded the resounding voice of Brassore as he turned to Z'har and fixed the young elf with a steely gaze, "for you the danger is still greater. It is no accident that out of the nearly twelve hundred souls of Skyfall, you Z'har are the only elf. Ever since the founding of the world, elves sought to remained set apart from the world. Their great and wondrous cities are often shut to all races, save of course the dwarves. Though we dwarves have tried to coax them from their forest domains to interact more readily with the other races, the elves will not relent. Even now, so few elven communities do business with outsiders, that many have begun to think of them as myth, or worse."

With these words, Brassore stood and walked to where Z'har sat, his eyes never leaving the elf's own. "You will face suspicion, fear, hatred and perhaps from a very few, adoration. I have watched your training these many years and know your skill with the blade, and other martial matters, is quite exceptional. But you will need to rely on your strength of will, discernment, and forbearance as you make your way through this world. I wish it were not so, but such is the state of Mythandria. I am sure your patience and virtue will be sorely tested, but have confidence that you are up for the challenge."

"So, what I'm hearing, is you have confidence that my sound wisdom and judgement will keep him safe from the foolishness of his young elven ways," quipped Niska as she playfully slapped Z'har on the back of the head. "That's funny, I was always taught that the wisdom of youth was fleeting," answered Z'har in his best imitation of Borack's voice. Their easy banter broke the tension that had been building within the audience hall and gave everyone cause for laughter. Although, for Z'har the truth in her words was yet another reason he was happy that she would be traveling by his side.

"I guess it is settled then," said Z'har after the moment of levity had passed. "Niska and I will prepare for a journey and leave upon the morrow. We'll break the news to everyone tonight and spend a night of fellowship in the Rainbow Meadow. I am sure most will understand, but I have concerns about Amatrix."

Turning to Pyrophane, Z'har continued. "She is only sixteen and yet is so full of anger. She tries to hide it, but it is plain to see. I often wonder if it has to do with the absence of our parents. I fear how she will take the news of our departure and that it will make things worse for her. She is only just now beginning to explore her zin abilities but even with her limited mastery, her might is extraordinary. What calamity would be let loose, if she were to lose control of her temper and her power at the same time."

"I know what you mean," said Niska who was involved in the most recent mishap with Amatrix's abilities during a training session. "Pyrophane, speak with Beryl and Ram and ask them to hang close to Amatrix in our absence. They are the closest of the Fallowsheirs to her age and she always seems to be in brighter spirits when they are around." To this she received a nod from Pyrophane.

She then turned to the head of the Sky Guard before saying, "First Commander Radelerz, if you feel it is prudent, can you instruct Ghost Hound to partner her with them for purposes of training and on any assignments?" Radelerz gave the burvore a nod of approval and said, "That shouldn't be a problem."

The meeting soon ended and Pyrophane joined Niska and Z'har as they headed back to The Fallows (the name given to the large track of land that was granted to Borack Fallows by Brassore nearly eighty years ago).

That evening, the makeshift family had a great feast of roast venison stewed with chunks of onions, potatoes and carrots and seasoned with various herbs and spices grown from the small garden they maintained on the property. Many laughs and a few tears were shared around bites of sticky honey bread and fluffy banana pudding washed down by spiced milk and strawberry flavored fusions; a drink comprised of water infused with the juices from berries or other fruit resulting in a sweet, full-bodied taste.

After the meal, Z'har bid Bodica and Zion to join the festivities. The massive hounds appeared from a barely discernable smoke emanating from Z'har's enchanted tattoo. They wagged their tails happily and pounced on the Fallowsheir siblings with pure delight. The evening was made all the livelier as the family engaged in a game of Hide & Don't Eat, as each of the Fallowsheirs scattered across their estate, seeking a place to hide from the stalking chaga hounds. One by one, the hounds hunted down their prey and slobbered them with wet licks. Of course, the game was never as easy but no less fun, when the siblings had to find the hounds, whose magical abilities made them truly hard to detect.

The family played late into the night, but at last laid

down to rest. Safely within the borders of Skyfall, they had no need for a watch. However, Pyrophane and the older Fallowsheirs knew that their time of peace may soon be coming to an end, as darkness gloomed on the horizon.

In the morning, Niska and Z'har received a package from Mihoko. Although she was not able to ascertain the specific location of the mysterious child from his dreams, Mihoko was able to point them in a northeasterly direction as she sensed their path would draw them into the Archstone Range. She provided several maps showing various regions outside of the Valley of Shale. Her note indicated she would continue to seek out more information and that the two should travel to Sunder's Dawn. There, they should look up her cousin Faldrin Fellsgrip who runs Faldrin's Anvil. Faldrin is knowledgeable about the region and may be able to provide further clarity about their quest. If she learns any new details, she will send a missive to Faldrin.

After saying their goodbyes, and loaded with provisions for the long road ahead, Z'har and Niska strolled out of Skyfall with Bodica and Zion as their only companions. Z'har felt a tightness in his chest as they passed Skyfall's borders. It had surely not been the first time he had been away from Skyfall, but this parting had the feeling of finality that he hoped was only irrational fear. He glanced at Niska and could tell from her silence, that she harbored similar concerns. And yet, the pleas of a child and the potential of discovering, called them forth and strengthened their resolve with every step.

Chapter 2:
The Awakened Tempest

The orc's blade sank into the exposed flank of a fleeing Cholulan warrior, mere breaths before being blasted away by a mighty bolt of arcane energy that tore a hole in its chest and similarly doomed six other orcs as it snaked through the enemy's ranks. Five warriors with sun-bronzed skin, leather garb, and feathers adorning their long raven-black hair rushed to their comrade's aid, while others sent a barrage of arrows that scattered the knot of orcs, goblins and ogres who were holding this particular stretch of terrain.

Cavazos Kimi breathed a small sigh of relief as he saw the young warrior stagger into the safety of the reforming Cholulan line. Yet, even as he gazed over the field of combatants, the old gnome berated himself for not being able to do more. His body just didn't respond as it once had. "Enough blathering, old man. Time to get to work," he scolded himself as he hefted his wondrous mace and moved to circumvent the bulk of warriors, with an eye on reaching the top of the bluff, where the enemy's banner waved in a slight breeze.

"The spirits of air have blessed us this day," came a

familiar voice as Adsila waded through the ranks of Cholulans to stride by her uncle's side. "That dust storm wreaked havoc on the enemy encampment last night. Without that confusion, I fear we would not be doing as well as we are. Even still, this battle will be a close thing. So, I says to myself, what would Born in Secret do, and sure enough I find you intent on cutting off the head of the snake. Not a bad plan uncle, but you know we couldn't let you have all the fun," finished Adsila as she swept blood and gore from her tomahawks, and used some of it to reinforce the lines of warpaint zigzagging their way across her cherubic face.

Cavazos spared a moment to cast an appreciative smile on Adsila, and her Fox Bloods (a small band of young warriors that were rapidly making a name for themselves during this period of turmoil that beset all of Chaluk'Sen). Fourteen of the braves joined Adsila and checked and rechecked their gear as they followed their leader around the main body of combatants. Cavazos knew more Fox Bloods were heading in their direction, but were less easily seen. They were either covered by magic or simply by the mastery of their own stealth. He did not speak any words, as there was no need to do so. The hill which they approached contained a heavy contingent of enemy, perhaps fifty strong who stood guard around their leader, the largest brawn Cavazos had ever seen. This would not be an easy fight, but it was one that needed to be finished here and now, if only to give the People (a term the various Cholulan tribes used to reinforce their unity of purpose and spirit) a precious few days of rest before others sought to test their resolve during the plague that ravaged Chaluk'Sen.

The small group had successfully trekked around the main battle, only facing minor resistance from the few enemy stragglers that stumbled upon their path and soon were sent to their final arbitration before Yen-Lo, the God of Judgment. Before them was an open field of more than one hundred yards, where their approach would hardly go unnoticed. Cavazos raised his hand, and the Fox Bloods instantly fell still and silent. The old gnome pulled his hair back into a bun, lamenting that he saw more gray than black in his hands, before tying it off with a sash from his belt. Once done, he let out a determined breath before standing to his full two-foot-eleven inches and whispering, "I will conceal our presence with a spell."

"And I'll create a distraction," Adsila interjected, her wicked grin promising swift death to their enemies. "The Wing and the Shadow?" she inquired as she began to unravel a large black feather nearly hidden within her thick mane of black hair.

"Why Adsila, it's almost as if we have done this before," responded Cavazos with a hearty chuckle. To the rest of the small unit he said, "When the magic takes effect and the feather flies, you must be quick across the field. I do not know if the enemy will be able to see through my magic but know at least some of them will fall victim to it. However, best not to leave matters to chance, aye?" With that, Cavazos cleared his mind and reached out to the Shadow Sea. After all these years, the magic waiting there seemed to seek him out like an old friend. As always, he gained vigor from his connection to the Great Flow and easily shaped the currents to wash invisibility upon his allies.

Trusting in the strength of her uncle's spell casting, Adsila stepped to the front of the line. She looked back on her warriors, assured that the enemies could not physically see them and determined to help cover any physical signs of their passage. Smearing the black feather with enemy blood that coated her armor, Adsila whispered a command to activate the feather's enchantment before throwing it into the air. The feather flitted into the air and disappeared, only to reappear about halfway across the field. Upon its appearance, the feather began to split into ghost-like apparitions. Within the next few heartbeats, the figures congealed into the very real form of a large murder of crows. Cavazos estimated that the flock contained perhaps two hundred birds and was pleased to see them speed across the distance, taking a circular path so they smashed into the enemy line from the opposite direction of his small force.

"The Luck be with you," he bellowed to his companions who was running even as the words left his mouth. "And to you, old man," he silently intoned as his short legs pumped to get him clear of the field and into the enemy's midst.

When the small band was about twenty yards away, Cavazos smiled as he saw the chaos the crows were causing. It is true they did not pose a significant threat to the warriors on the hill, but their wings, beaks and talons held the enemy's attention. The diversion became even more effective as the crows coalesced into eleven humanoid birdmen, that landed on the opposite side of the hill and charged their flummoxed foes. Just as Cavazos was beginning his ascent up the hill, he caught sight of a few arrows speeding towards the hill-locked enemy. Obviously Adsila had magically contacted the other members of the Fox Bloods and instructed them to aid in the assault. Their plan appeared to be working perfectly as none of the mongrels (orcs, hobgoblins, and brawns) seemed to even glance in their direction.

Cavazos was breathing heavily as he reached the zenith of the hill. He quickly scanned the scene before him, desperate to locate the leader of this invasion force. With all the chaos, it should have been more difficult to make out individual warriors, but such was not the case as he beheld the battle-scarred brawn bellowing orders even as she dispatched attackers with abandon. The purple-skinned bipedal humanoid stood fully twelve feet tall, with a mouth full of razor-sharp teeth and a massive tongue that shot out to slam into one of the summoned bird creatures. Her unfortunate victim instantly seized up and fell over in a paralytic state and was left exposed for the hobgoblin that moved in a blur as he easily cleaved the creature's head from its body. The brawn then turned her reptilian gaze upon the approaching enemy and laughed with relish, calling out something in Mud Tongue that had the others on her side laughing even as they prepared themselves to meet the coming onslaught.

Just then, the front line of Cavazos' force hit the enemy from the rear. To a casual observer it would have looked as if the Cholulan warriors merely appeared within the enemy ranks as their invisibility lapsed whenever one committed an attack upon a foe. Adsila was at the head of the line and sank her tomahawk into the flank of a large orc, before stepping past to severe the leg of the next enemy at the knees. Realizing the attack was coming from both sides, the brawn shouted orders in Mud Tongue, that had half of her force turning to face the new threat. As she turned her attention to the new foes, the brawn sent out a wicked-looking whip that sparkled with necrotic energy and wrapped around the neck of a Cholulan female five paces to the left of the still invisible Cavazos. With a savage tug of the whip, the Cholulan's skeleton was ripped out of her body, leaving a sickening mass of blood and flesh to wash over the field.

Okay, don't get hit by that creature whose four times your height, Cavazos thought to himself as his body infused with energy and strength from another spell, he cast on himself. Picking his way as quickly as caution would allow, through the combatants, Cavazos at last stood in front of the massive brawn that stood at least four times his height and was sending her whip to crack against the magical shield of a Cholulan halfling, that buckled under the weight of the blow, but did not fall.

Without hesitation, Cavazos raised Tempest, his powerfully enchanted mace, and brought it down with all the might he could muster. His aim was true, and the large brawn was caught completely unprepared as pain wracked her body as all of the bones in her left foot shattered under the weight of Cavazos' blow. The surprising pain had her involuntarily doubling over, which was just what Cavazos had desired. *Thunder*, he commanded in his mind as he swung Tempest into an upward arc to connect solidly with the jaw of the brawn. Upon impact, the sound of thunder echoed across the field as a percussive blast rocked the brawn, blowing off her lower jaw as many of her upper teeth shattered. *Lightning*, Cavazos thought as he aimed the Tempest's head at the brawn that was falling backward. Instantly, a bolt of lightning leapt from the mace and hammered into the brawn, extending her fall and sending her sprawling down the hill.

Not too shabby, Cavazos thought as he prepared to follow his foe to make sure the job was well and truly done. However, the thought had barely formed in his mind as a blow hit him from behind, causing sparks of sand and clay to fly from his head. Pain and dizziness warred in his body as Cavazos stumbled in a daze. He was vaguely aware that were it not for the protection of his spell, the blow surely would have ended him. Yet given the amount of blood that began to trickle from the wound and seeing the blurred form of an attacker swiftly approaching, Cavazos thought that things were going from bad to worse. No time to dawdle, old man, Cavazos berated himself as he squared his shoulder to meet the hobgoblin's charge.

"Not today, you grimy son of a horse humper!" roared an enraged Adsila as she stepped in the hobgoblin's path and swiped at him with her tomahawk, which hit only air as the speedy hobgoblin easily sidestepped her attack and delivered a vicious strike to her left arm with his short sword. The next few moments seemed to mesh into one breath as Cavazos watched the hobgoblin, obviously aided by some increased speed spell, seem to toy with Adsila, opening cut after cut, trying to break through her defenses to deliver a killing blow.

Frustrated and exhausted, Adsila clasped her tomahawk with both hands and when she pulled them apart, had an identical tomahawk in each hand. Cavazos had seen that particular enchantment of her weapon before but was mystified when Adsila leapt into the air and swung her right-hand weapon horizontal to the ground before releasing it. As she hit the ground, the tomahawk disappeared. Adsila breathed in a steadying breath as she turned towards the approaching hobgoblin, summoning another twin tomahawk so that she now had two deadly weapons, which she plied with uncanny skill in an all-out assault on the hobgoblin. Their weapons range in unison as Adsila hammered the hobgoblin from the left, attempting to expose a crack in his defense. But such was not to be the case, and the hobgoblin laughed aloud as he scored a deep gash on Adsila's left side before zooming past. Yet Adsila, grimacing in pain, winked at the hobgoblin, whose confused expression froze forever as his neck collided with the enchanted blade extended in the air. The momentum of the hobgoblin's charge, and the sharpness of the blade, severed tendons and bone, sending the hobgoblin's head tumbling to the ground. The, now visible, tomahawk winked out of existence and Adsila could feel its weight once again added to the blade in her hand.

"Nice trick," said Cavazos whose head was only just clearing from the pain induced haze. The old gnome glanced cautiously around before making his way over to his niece to shower them both in a healing spell. He could see that the battle for the hill was turning in their favor as more of the Fox Bloods joined the fray.

"It's not over yet," spoke Adsila as she wearily turned towards the loud growl coming from up ahead. She involuntarily took a step back as the body of a human Cholulan came soaring through the air, followed by the pondering figure of the brawn leader. In her left hand, the brawn held a shakaran female by the neck, giving a savage twist of her wrist that broke the neck of the struggling Cholulan. As the body fell to the ground, the brawn raised her hand and called forth a stream of bubbling acid that rushed from her towards the advancing enemy.

The blast rolled over Cavazos with no effect, but Adsila and most of the Fox Bloods were not so fortunate. Angry red blistered bubbled on their flesh and several fell due to the damage of the spell. Without uttering a word, Cavazos called upon a spell, causing arms of earth to explode from the ground to encase the feet of the brawn. Another gesture of his hands, caused two more tendrils to wrap around the enraged brawn's arms, pulling her upright with all four appendages stretched out. Closing his hands into fists, Cavazos pulled them toward his chest, before violently thrusting them at the brawn. The earth responded to Cavazos' command and a large spike of rock and gravel shot out to burst through the brawn's chest, ending her struggle forever.

After several more desperate minutes of fighting, the Fox Bloods killed the enemy and secured the hill. A momentary cheer of jubilation rose from some of their lips, and Cavazos noted the forlorn look upon Adsila's face. Knowing how much his niece enjoyed battle, Cavazos put his hands on her shoulders and said, "Don't worry, little Blossom, there's more." With that, he turned her around to gaze down the hill, towards the main battle line.

A wry smile curved Adsila's delicate lips as she beheld the field below. The Cholulans were poised to win the day, and the invading mongrels could sense the change. Many of them were fleeing the field, scattering in all different directions, but a force of maybe eighty were headed straight towards the hill. The leader of the approaching mob, a bulging brawn with greenish-gray skin, looked up and glowered at them with a look that promised something worse than death. Though Adsila was no great expert on brawns, she thought this particular specimen bore a distinct likeness of the dead one now lying in their midst. Gauging the distance of the approaching force, Adsila figured they only had a couple of moments to prepare to meet the combatants.

Pulling out a vial, Adsila quickly downed a strong Potion of Vitality. "Drink em if you got em," she said to the warriors around her. The hill is ours and I'll be buggered by a half-eaten sloth's sow before I let that rabble run us off it." She shook yet more blood from her tomahawk and started motioning where she wanted her warriors to be. "Circle up, archers in the middle. Let fly as soon as they are within range and show Pawnee, the great Goddess of the Hunt, why she chose to grace Chaluk'Sen with her favor." As warriors rushed to heed her call, Adsila's words were met with a resounding chorus of, "The Huntsman's will gives us the strength to kill, and sends us this way is our prey for the day!"

No sooner had the first of the advancing foes touched foot to hill, than a swarm of arrows and ranged spells came showering down upon them. Several fell dead, or were pulled up from a grievous wound, but many more came spilling up the hill. As Adsila gazed down at the approaching force, her heart pounded with excitement and the tomahawk seemed to hum in her hand. Standing beside her, Cavazos reached his will into the Shadow Sea and cast a spell that caused forty-two jagged spikes of earth to erupt all around the hill, running enemies through with ease. This slowed the mad dash as those behind the first ranks smashed into their comrades or fought desperately to avoid the deadly projectiles. Before the enemy could regain its bearings, Cavazos threw Tempest high into the air. When the weapon reached its zenith, he mentally commanded *Lighting Storm* and watched as the weapon responded by sending blinding tendrils of lightning lancing down in an arc to soak the enemy in blazing agony, killing ten of the approaching enemy, and scorching still more.

Due to the quick demise of so many of their allies, coupled with the fact that the advancing Cholulan force was getting closer, the mob of mongrels lost any hope of retaking the hill and began to seek the quickest route to extract themselves from the field of death. Most fled in sheer panic, but a group of gnolls formed around a large female as they carefully chose the safest route out of harm's way. An angry snarl left the lips of the mighty brawn warrior that looked up the hill and lifted his hand to perform a profane gesture. The creature shouted something, but Adsila was too far away to make it out. However, she could surmise it as a threat of vengeance. This had her laughing as she hurled her tomahawk in the brawn's direction. Adsila was only slightly surprised as the enchanted weapon cracked against a magical barrier surrounding the brawn, before materializing back in her waiting hand. The sneering brawn spat on the ground, before stepping sideways into a portal of his own making. Within moments, three of the brawn's companions also stepped into the portal and were whisked away to safety.

Adsila knew enough about brawns to know that this one might pose a threat in the future and so she determined to seek him out at her earliest convenience to resolve the issue once and for all. But today, she and the Fox Bloods had work to do. Cavazos knew her heart and gave her a silent nod and waved away her concerns for his safety. "I may be old, but I don't need a wetnurse to look after me. May the spirits bless you on this hunt," he finished as he gently shoved her towards the fleeing enemy. In response, Adsila turned to her warriors, raised her tomahawk into the air, and released a savage war cry that was quickly picked up by the rest of the Fox Bloods, and a few other Cholulans that were even now overtaking the enemy. "Let's go teach these wretched mongrels that it is not but folly to test the will of Chaluk'Sen!" With that, the Fox Bloods went on the search for prey.

Later that night, Cavazos sat in a ring of Cholulan elders, drinking spiced milk that had been heated to fend off the chill of the spring evening. He watched with pride as young warriors danced and sang around a mighty campfire set in the middle of a vast field of teepees. The traditional dance was led by Ehawee, an onataha whose name means *Laughing Maiden*. Onatahas (often called shamans in other cultures) were highly respected women responsible for the spiritual well-being of the People. While Ehawee was young, she had earned the respect of all members of the Snokomish Clan, due to her tireless efforts to combat the rigors of the plague that ushered so many Cholulans to the grave. Rumor had it, that she had been asked to speak before the Zonta Onawa, a Tribal Council wherein all the clans of the Kodiak Tribe would gather and present updates to the Migisi'Oya, the tribe's High Chief.

Donning a ceremonial headdress, symbolizing the great Kodiak bear, Ehawee open wounds on her arms and those of the dancing warriors. The blood was allowed to flow freely as a gift to the spirits of earth and wind, animals and ancestors, whose wisdom and aid had served the Cholulans for millennia. Cavazos did not need to open his mind to the Spirit Realm to know their words were being accepted. He could see that the blood offering of the people was being absorbed by attending spirits as not one drop of the precious substance hit the ground.

Cavazos was astonished to find tears in his eyes as he did not realize how much he truly missed this ceremonial dance. He had spent most of the last hundred years in lands beyond Chaluk'Sen. He believed that he could best serve the People, by spreading their values to other cultures and making allies that could be relied upon during times of trouble. About a year ago, he received a summons from Kisecawchuck, the Nadia'Opa of the Snokomish Clan. The Clan Chief, whose name means Day Spirt, was calling all clan members back home to help defend the People during this terrible time. The old gnome was one of many thousands of Cholulans that responded to similar pleas from the multitude of Clan Chiefs across the great expanse of Chaluk'Sen. While he had been home from time to time, this was first time in a long while he had spent so many months with his people and he realized that the fellowship of other Cholulans was a loss he had not truly reconned with.

Cavazos lost himself in time as he basked in the joys of his fellows and gazed up into the night's sky. The white sphere of the Frozen Moon hung heavy in the sky, as its smaller counterpart, the Blood Moon could be seen blazing her path across the heavens. But at last, his bones reminded him that he was not as young as he once was, and so Cavazos said his goodbyes to those around him and made his way to the warmth of his teepee. Along the way, he gave a small wave to Adsila who was playing a game of Bear Talons with several Fox Bloods since the ceremonial dance was over. The young gnome shot Cavazos a sly smile as she collected gem fragments as payment for her winnings.

By the time Cavazos made it back to his teepee, night had full mastery of the hour. His mind and heart were awash with thought and emotion as he mechanically stoked the heated rocks, activating their enchantment and infusing his shelter with warmth. He then pulled up a chair to the small fold-out circular table and ate a late repast of meat and cheese. After taking time to send his consciousness into the Shadow Sea and thank his patron for sharing the knowledge of his spells, Cavazos stripped down to his breaches and climbed beneath the warm furs, allowing sleep to envelop him with the comfort of long companionship.

His dream started as they often did. Cavazos was again a youth, running with other Cholulan children through the woods. On this day, they were more excited than usual as they flitted through the tree draped field, looking for signs of the Catawal pack that was rumored to be in the area. While the large felines had been domesticated by some tribes of the People Cavazos' clan, the Snokomishs, had no such mounts. Indeed, it was rare for any of the youths to see the beasts whose glasslike bones carried so mighty an enchantment that they were commonly shaped into wondrous items of power.

The woods were thick that day, and young Cavazos quickly lost sight of the other children. His footsteps faltered as he sought out any tell-tale sign of their passing, but none were to be found. Furtive movements from the left caused Cavazos to look that way in time to catch a faint glimpse of a blurred white shape dashing further into a denser copse of trees. Without moving, Cavazos found himself standing within those tall trees that grew even larger as they extended their twisted branches in his direction. Cavazos had to scramble to stay ahead of their questing digits as fear rapidly spread within his fast-beating heart. Too late, did he notice the massive tree that appeared suddenly in his path, with writhing vines that grasped him in a terrible embrace before ushering him into its waiting maw.

"Help, help!" shouted a horrified young Cavazos as all the world was drawn to blackness.

An echo sounded somewhere in the distance. It was his voice, but somehow not. "Help, help" shouted the horrified young child in a manner that spoke of pure bitterness and utter hopelessness. Overcome by the loss that hung on those words with a noose, young Cavazos pushed his way through the grasping darkness, his fingers mired in muck and dank despair. Before long, his tiny limbs began to feel the weight of the world and, and his steps slowed, and…

"Help me, help me please!" words spoken in the darkness that grabbed him with the strength of a giant and pulled young man Cavazos out of the darkness and into a watery wonderland. From the way the moss glowed, even under water, Cavazos could tell he was in an unterland river. The strong currents tugged him along and he lost himself in the buzz of colors and shapes that drifted swiftly by. Something stirred in the deep, and Cavazos could feel the dark tendrils of a forgotten monstrosity wriggling in his direction. Terror, rich as the mightiest vein of gold, gripped his very soul and spurred him to fight through the growing current to breach the surface and scramble up the darkened beach. Sand and dirt intermingled under his fingers, and soon the round blades of the unterland grass rubbed against his numb fingers, pointing him towards a patch of gray outlined within the utter blackness of the unterland environs.

Stumbling into the gray, old man Cavazos found himself standing in a long hallway, lined with closed doors. Looking back, he glimpsed a massive shape lumbering out of the water and dashing towards him, only to have a door slam shut, locking it and the darkness out.

"Are you here to help me?" pleaded a small half-elf child. The young vlel looked disheveled and exasperated. "Please help me. I have been calling for so long. I thought someone had answered me before, but then I think I awoke the beast, the monster out there." As the child's words bubbled out of her mouth images flashed across Cavazos' mind.

He saw her in an opulent room, shackled to a large human who sneered in her direction as he yanked the shackles, causing cuts to open on her wrists. Even as she gasped in pain, an elf appeared from the shadows freeing her from the shackles and holding her with care. The elation on the child's face was palpable, but soon became fear and anguish as the elf, suddenly at arms-length, plunged a sword through her heart. Blood flooded Cavazos' vision as the vlel once again looked up from her confined room and whispered. "Help me, please. Darkness is coming and I am so afraid."

The words of the child were lost in a cacophony of sound and sights as the walls of the hallway were peeled back, revealing the dark inky tendrils of a gargantuan shape rising out of an ancient tomb. As the tendrils of darkness filled the room, a deeply resonant voice sounded in Cavazos' heart as his brain was torn asunder and a cry of pain and terror escaped his lips.

"Ah, Leloni, there you are..." the voice stated even as a hand yanked on Cavazos' pinky finger and a familiar voice called him from the Plane of Dreams, to awake sweating and shouting within the confines of his teepee.

Exasperated and full of fear, Cavazos threw off his damp fur blankets and jumped up, preparing to defend himself. "Be at peace, old friend." came a voice tinged with an enchantment that soothed Cavazos' strained nerves. The old gnome's sanity slowly found his body as his eyes watched the remnant of a dream catcher burning in the air. His gaze slowly tracked down towards the ground to gaze upon a concerned bulldog standing warily beside the nine-inch figure of Itsumata Jahdon.

"Itsumi?" queried Cavazos as he looked at the brownie in surprise. The diminutive figure whose large oval eyes filled most of her elongated head looked up at the much larger gnome and gave him a reassuring smile. Her delicate frame seemed to fill the room as a portion of her inner power seeped into this reality.

"I'm afraid you made quite a fuss," Itsumata stated indicating the noise coming from outside of the teepee. As if on cue, Adsila burst through the structure's opening with tomahawk drawn, searching for any sign of a threat to her dear uncle. Outside, other warriors mustered ready to act. Recognition shot across her eyes like an arrow loosed as she spied the seated bulldog and her curious rider.

"Uncle are you okay?" she asked, slowly advancing towards Cavazos' bed while giving the brownie and her familiar as wide a birth as the teepee would allow.

"I am well," responded Cavazos, his voice dripping with resignation and more than a bit of embarrassment. "Would you believe this old man can still get scared by the stuff of dreams? But that is the truth of it. I must really be past my prime to have reverted back to the days of youth when a mother is needed to calm my trembling heart." With that, Cavazos picked himself up from the ground and sat heavily in the chair by the table. He irritably waved away the questing eyes from the warriors outside who were peaking in to see if their blades would be needed once again this day.

Seeing his discomfort, Adsila went to the flap and explained that all was well, before returning to stand by her uncle's side. "Apologies, Born in Secret, for my intrusion. Some of the guys and I were finally headed to get some much-needed sleep, when we heard the…," How could she cover the fact that Cavazos was screaming like a four-year-old that had taken his first tumble from horseback? "…*commotion* coming from your teepee. Fearing the mongrels had somehow found a way past our defenses, I rushed in without thinking."

"Pish, posh," scolded the tiny figure of Itsumata as she deftly scaled the table's legs and soon stood on its surface, glancing between Adsila and Cavazos. "You both acted appropriately given the perspectives you both had on tonight's events."

Turning to Cavazos, she continued, "Fear of what you witnessed in the Dream Plane is wisdom, not a sign of cowardice. In fact, Mother Midnight has sensed a growing threat emanating from that plane and seeping into ours. She is already dealing with machinations from several of the Shadow Born lords and can ill afford the time to investigate this matter on her own. She bid me to find, that you might ferret out the exact nature of the threat which she has sensed, and you have just experienced."

"Mother Midnight, huh." Cavazos stated as he thought about his Shadow Born Benefactor. Avri'Nvar, more commonly known as Mother Midnight, was an ancient being of the Shadow Sea denizen who entered into lasting compacts with other beings, trading her knowledge of spells and other arcana for their services in pursuit of her designs.

"Why did she pick me?" asked Cavazos who stood up and began packing his things for the journey that he knew he must take. "Why didn't she go to one of her other warlocks?" he finished, referring to any of the other mages that had entered such a contract with Mother Midnight. While he did not know all of them, he was certain a few of them would be much better equipped to deal with that thing he saw in his dream. *Why send an old man whose footsteps were closer to the grave than the crib?*

"Enough of that uncle," interrupted Adsila whose

words of admonishment were buttressed when Itsumata chimed in.

"You know why. You may wish to fool yourself, but you're still one of the most powerful mages around. Besides, I can hear the eagerness in your steps that bely your sour demeaner. More time on the road would do you good. You were not meant to live the life of a hermit. Your time to rest has not come yet."

"But," started Cavazos, not willing to so easily give up the fight. "…I am needed here. The People are still under great distress due to the plague, the dangers of the cadda-ja'lyn, and the threats from outsiders that seek to test our might."

"It is true the plague has brought us low, but word is spreading that a cure has been found from the blood of a halfling from the Masai Tribe. That was apparently before some group calling themselves Wahuru was instrumental in discerning the cause of the *caddaja'lyn*. While it is unclear what their exact role was, they did play some part in the great battle within the unterland territory of the Sinikit Tribe. Since then, the threat of the caddaja'lyn has been greatly reduced. And as for the mongrels and other outside invaders? Well," she said bringing her tomahawk to her lips and giving it a gentle kiss, "…that's what the People have me for."

"Well, I can't argue with that," responded Cavazos who only then realized he had fully packed his traveling gear and stood with the heavy backpack thrown over his shoulders. "My dear sister would have been so proud of the warrior you have become. You honor her spirit, and I must likewise honor my oath to Mother Midnight. So, where do I start Itsumi?" he finished, directing this last part to the brownie who was looking at him with the look of a mother who patiently waited for her foolish child to exhaust all his excuses only to end up doing what she wanted in the first place.

Reaching into the extradimensional space of her tiny splinter-sac, Itsumata withdrew a large pouch that was nearly as large as she. With casual ease, she tossed the pouch to Cavazos, who surmised its contents due to the sound of jingling from within.

"This will help get you started." Itsumata began, as she jumped off the table and landed smoothly beside the waiting hound, who towered over her. "The full knowledge of your quest was not given to me, and I cannot see where your path will lead. Bella and I were sent to get your started, so the question is, where is it that you would like to go?"

Thinking of the dark creature and frightened child within his dream, Cavazos knew the journey ahead would be dangerous and so he would need the aid of some long-time companions. Suddenly, he felt every bit of his two hundred and sixty years. He walked over and embraced his niece, placing a gentle kiss on her forehead before saying, "Well Little Blossom, it looks like you're going to have to make all those kills without me. Keep those Fox Bloods in line and those blades sharp until next we meet."

Released from the embrace, Adsila withdrew a small vial from her belongings. From it, she poured drops of blood onto her fingers. She then traced a bloody circle on her uncle's forehead before intoning the words to an ancient prayer that beseeched the spirit of the Kodiak bear, (their tribe's sacred totem spirit) to watch over Cavazos and to bring him safely home.

After embracing once more, Adsila followed Cavazos and Itsumata outside and watched as the brownie climbed on the Bella's back. Runes concealed under the bulldog's light brown fur began to glow as she grew large enough so that Cavazos could join the brownie on her back.

"Where to?" asked Itsumata after Cavazos was settled.

"To the Archstone Range," Cavazos answered feeling a brief flutter of excitement for the adventure to come. "I have some friends in Sunder's Down, that might be interested in seeing where this trail will lead us."

"You heard him girl," said Itsumata as she stroked the fur behind Bella's ears. The bulldog walked through the large Cholulan encampment, apparently shielded by some enchantment, as none seem to register their passage. Once beyond the camp's perimeter Bella started off at a steady jog, that soon became a full out run as she sprang wings and jumped into the air, silently soaring to the lands far to the south.

Cavazos had traveled with this pair many times in the past and was not surprised as downy feathers grew from the exposed arms of the seated brownie. Looking down, past Bella's fur that curled tightly around his legs, locking him in place, Cavazos gazed fondling upon the sweeping lands of Chaluk'Sen. His pride for his people lingered long after the many groves of trees, rolling hills and bubbling streams fell from view as the flying trio breached the clouds and sped towards destiny.

Chapter 3:
UNFRIENDLY WELCOME

"Alright lassie, we're ready to head out. You sure you're wantin to be stopping at this here hamlet?" asked Litlax, the halfling leader of the caravan Ferika had been traveling with for the last few weeks. "The way I hear it, yon Sunder's Dawn is only for them that aren't up to no good. Don't seem like a fitting spot for one such as yourself if ye don't mind me sayin such."

"Thanks for your concern, Litlax," responded the young human as she pulled her backpack off the load wagon. "It's been more than a few years since last I was through this way, and while the hamlet sure has grown, I'm thinking that it won't have changed too much. I'll be fine; besides I'll be meeting with some folks before continuing on. So, I don't plan on being here too long." As Ferika began to walk towards the distant hamlet, she hollered back, "I pray that The Luck guide your steps down a profitable path." To which, Litlax responded, "The Luck has ever been in my favor, and I'm sure he'll smile on yourself as well."

The sun was in its zenith, bringing a thaw to the chill of the early spring morning, as Ferika drew closer to Sunder's

Dawn. Maybe she had been gone longer than she thought, because the place was much larger than she remembered. Where once there were just a few log cabins, a single general store and a well-maintained, but pitifully small inn, there now stood a sprawling community surrounded by a large timber wall. From her vantage at the top of the hill, Ferika could see the walls around Sunder's Dawn were not entirely complete. Work was still taking shape on a few sections further on the western end, away from the gate she was approaching. She scanned the many buildings, some made of stone but most still constructed of timber. The hamlet was abuzz with activity as horse drawn carts zigged and zagged along rough-hewn dirt roads before gaining a smoother purchase on some of the newer cobblestone paths in a section of the city with larger houses, opulent shops, and a more orderly layout.

Closer to the town's gates, Ferika joined in the line of people waiting to get into Sunder's Dawn. Most appeared to be local farmers or hunters, looking to make a profit by selling their wares in the hamlet. Four guards stood at the gate, allowing most people to enter with only a cursory examination, while stopping others for questioning.

One of the guards, a heavy-set human female with wide hips and a fresh-looking scar along her left shoulder, stepped in front of Ferika. "Well met traveler. I don't think I've seen you here before." The guard stated in an amiable manner. However, Ferika saw her huge right hand rested on the hilt of a sheathed sword. "What's your business in Sunder's Dawn?"

"I am actually here just planning on meeting some old friends at a place called the Land Duck Inn," Ferika responded, opening wide her hands to show that she was no threat. "I haven't been here in many years and am amazed at the progress you guys have made. Last time, I was through there were only a couple of families living here, but now look at what you have done. I'm quite impressed."

Ferika words had their desired effect as the guard seemed to relax a bit. Her hand strayed from her weapon as she gestured towards the city. The pride in her voice was evident as she said, "Yeah, it has been a pretty hard road, but we Dawners are nothing if not tough. I stopped you because we don't get too many people coming in on their own, plus there aren't many fire heads in Sunder's Dawn, so you really stand out."

"Fire heads? I'm not…" Ferika began but was cut off as the guard raised a meaty hand to indicate Ferika's mop of red hair.

"It's a pretty look, but one that might get you in trouble. Just don't go wanderin down any alleys or anything. Being alone, there's no telling the kind of stuff that could happen to you." The guard checked Ferika's eyes, a look that all women knew too well, before continuing. "Your best bet on getting to the Land Duck Inn is to stick to the main thoroughfare," she pointed, indicating the main road leading away from the gate. "This'll get you to the Starbright Market. Cut through the market and you're just a few blocks from your destination. Any of the vendors at the market will be able to give you directions from there."

"Thanks for your help," Ferika said to the guard who gave her a polite nod, before stepping up to question a rough looking half orc further down the line. The orceen was leading two massive oxen that seemed to be about to buckle under the weight of the load within their wagon. As she stepped into Sunder's Dawn, Ferika heard the female guard exclaim, "Buntok, it has been too long. I thought one of them wild creatures had surely put an end to you…" The rest of their conversation was quickly drowned out by the rush of noise and the hustle bustle of the activity that soon overwhelmed Ferika's senses.

Ferika walked deeper into Sunder's Dawn, following the road that was identified by a sign written in Oromo, Wood Tongue, Dwarf Tongue and two languages Ferika couldn't read. The sign marked the street as First Road, which the young human didn't give any points for originality. But staying on the beaten path was easy enough and so Ferika had time to take in the sights and sounds. As with many places she had been, Sunder's Dawn was home to a variety of people. She saw dwarves laughing and joking with a cohort of gnomes and halflings, while a small singing group composed of a shakaran, a shorn and two humans were set up along the street with a growing crowd listening intently. Most of the humans that she saw, were dark skinned but more than a few with pale skin could be seen flitting from place to place.

The architecture that buttressed First Road was predominantly new construction. Most were tall, two- or three-story establishments that hosted an assortment of businesses in one edifice. The business owners of Sunder's Dawn seemed to take great pride in maintaining the appearance of wealth as many of the shops were decorated with colorful signs, elegantly designed columns and fresh paint. But every now and then, Ferika could see signs that people were the same all over. She looked with minor annoyance to the top of one particularly tall building where someone had painted graffiti on the bell tower. Workers were carefully painting over the **XTG**, that had been painted in vibrant calligraphic letters. The workers seemed to be having some dispute over which shade of paint most closely matched the original color used to decorate the tower. *What a waste*, Ferika thought as she continued and finally came to a large open-air market, with a massive sign that read Starbright Market, carved into the side of an enormous boulder.

A myriad of shops lined every available space within the big square that was crisscrossed by a confusing network of walkways, which led from one vendor to another. Since there were many hours of daylight left, Ferika took her time looking at the wares from a few of the shops. While many items caught her attention, the teen couldn't help but purchase a star munch from a young vendor that did all he could to haggle her out of every silver. While she wound up paying three bronze pieces for the treat, she tipped the fellow a silver after taking her first bite of the gooey candy. Star munch candy was a staple throughout Midian, but the vendors of the Archstone Range seemed most adept at making it. The candy's hard outer shell was made of chocolate and crushed nuts, while the inside was a scrumptious cream made of coconut and various fruit blends.

Wanting to savor the experience, Ferika took a seat within one of the market's many eating stalls. The eating stalls were set up to resemble an actual building with four walls, tables, chairs and the like. The only thing missing was the roof, which allowed the afternoon sun to stream in, reflecting the light mood of the people enjoying their meals. After about fifteen minutes, Ferika finished her snack and was ready to move on, when she heard someone call out, "Hey you, does the grass match the vines?" This statement was followed by a smattering of laughter.

Ferika casually looked around, to see who had spoken and who he was speaking too. She was a bit surprised to see a handsome blond man strolling towards her. His lovely blue eyes nearly matched the color of the heavens after a light rain, and his smile was broad and mischievous.

"Uh, excuse me," Ferika responded in Wood Tongue. "I think you must have me mistaken with someone who would be stupid enough to consider that a smooth line." With that, she turned and started for the door of the eating stall. However, before she had taken two steps the man's hand grabbed her right wrist tightly and turned her to face him.

"Ah, come on sweet thing. Why don't you come and sit on Lorat's lap and tell me all about how naughty I am?" the man continued as he attempted to pull Ferika into an intimate embrace.

"I'm sorry, but you are not my type." Ferika calmly stated as she swiveled her wrist so the angle of her palm pushed against the man's thumb, finding the weak point of his hold and allowing Ferika to easily extricate herself from his grasp.

"Oh, I see," said the man, his smile disappearing, "You must be confused. That wasn't a request," he finished as he grabbed the girl by both shoulders and tried to bring her in for a kiss.

"I said NO!" shouted Ferika as she swiveled her hips, causing the man to overbalance as he attempted to maintain his grip on her shoulders. Ferika extended her right hand, with knuckles extended, and rammed it into the man's exposed neck. The man stepped back in pain, before shouting, "You stinkin whore!" and lunging at her with a fierce left-hand punch.

Ferika smoothly ducked into the man, easily coming up under his punch and using his own momentum to launch him over her small frame to slam into an empty table nearby. Ferika took several steps back, ready to meet the man with further aggression if he persisted. She was vaguely aware that many of the patrons had cleared out. Maybe it is time for me to do the same, she thought as she turned towards the door, only to discover it was blocked by a large man with dirty-blonde hair and a club in his hands.

"Ha, ha, ha," came the mocking laughter of Lorat, as he climbed to his feet and smeared blood from his left cheek, revealing a tattooed X that Ferika hadn't noticed before. "Well, you went and done it didn't you. It was just going to be me, but now you're going to have fun with all of us." As he finished, Ferika looked around and could see that six other men stood around the perimeter of the stall. One was closing the shutters to the stall's windows, while another was scratching at his crotch and shot her a sly wink. Two others looked downright bored, while one was trying hard to cover his obvious amusement at Lorat's discomfort.

"Look, I just want to go," said Ferika as she freed the quarterstaff from the straps on her back and silently called upon the magic of a spell that would harden her skin. She had no illusions that she would win but wasn't about to just stand there and take it. In fact, she was pretty sure she could gut at least four of them before the others overpowered her. *Oh gods, why is this happening?* Ferika thought, as she gritted her teeth against the encounter to come.

"What the…" came a sound from the door as the big man guarding it came stumbling past her, smashing a table as he attempted to catch himself.

In his place stood a tall human, perhaps around six foot five inches, whose lean frame was covered in skin so dark that it was nearly black. The man did not move, but let his eyes take in the entirety of the scene in front of him.

"Que pasa hermano?" came a voice as a shorter man

stepped into the stall to stand by the tall figure. This one was much shorter, perhaps five foot six inches.

"Oh, nothing much," said the first man as he casually walked further into the room, to stand a few paces from Ferika, who positioned herself to defend herself from this newcomer, should he become a threat. Seeing her concern, the black man raised his hands while shaking his head.

"It seems like these Xrs were looking to have a little fun with this young lady here." The way he said fun, as if the word were poison to his tongue, gave Ferika hope that he was not here to hurt her. Turning his back to Ferika, the man's deep voice rumbled out of him with the sound of waves crashing against a shore. "Perhaps young lady, we could help educate these boys on how a woman should be treated."

"Ah, then we're in luck hermano," said the other man as he walked over to stand in front of Lorat. His voice was light and full of merriment as he continued, "Here I was, having a hum drum day, when these Xr boys go and give us cause to play." The man's hands disappeared beneath the fabric of his gray and black poncho before reappearing with a blade in each.

"So, what is it Xrs? Do we have a problem?" asked the tall man, who stood poised but relaxed. Ferika could feel the unease of her attackers as they looked at each other like foxes that had been cornered.

"N.. no, there's no problem Bla…" Lorat began as he took several steps back, but quickly shut his mouth, amid audible gasps from his fellows. His eyes were saucers as he looked at the tall man and gulped loudly trying to coax saliva into a suddenly dry throat.

"Why hermano, I do believe he was about to call you Blackie. Were you about to call my brother Blackie?" asked the smaller man, punctuating his question by sending one of his blades across the distance to open up another stream of blood on his cheek.

"No," said the tall man with menace that seemed to suck the sunlight out of the room. "He wouldn't say that hermano because he knows that if he did, I'd crack his skull open and rip out his innards as food for the many rats that plague this place. So, what is it boy, you wanting to ensure the health of Sunder's Dawn's rodent population?"

With that, a spell must have been lifted, for the men that were so menacing just moments ago scrambled out of the stall and ran through the market as if the very hounds of Demmis were on their heels.

"Woo wee, look at them boys run." Laughed the shorter man as he retrieved his thrown blade and wiped off the blood before placing it back in his bandolier.

The taller man turned to Ferika with a smile on his face. He took several steps back before addressing her in that sonorous voice that threatened to drown her in its richness. "Apologies young lady, I'm sorry you had to experience such a crude display of machismo from some of the lesser men of this community. I imagine one day my brother and I are going to have to take steps to rid this place of ones such as those."

"Ah brother of mine, where are our manners," said the tall man as he went to upright one of the tables. "We have yet to introduce ourselves. My name," he started as he bent into an elegant bow, "is Mel Uhneen, and this" he said indicating the smaller fellow who also bowed, "is Mateo La'ahtyne. My brother and I have recently purchased a residence within this fair community. We have not spent much time in Sunder's Dawn as our duties often take us beyond the walls, but as with so many other places the criminal element within this community seems to believe they can act with impunity."

"So, it would seem," responded Ferika as the tension began to drain from her body. "My name is Ferika Feathertouch, and I was actually on my way to the Land Duck Inn before these Xrs, as you called them, began their harassment. I thank you both for intervening as I dread to think what would have happened otherwise."

Hearing the growing anxiety in Ferika's voice, Mateo stepped towards her and said, "The moment has passed, and you are safe. Yes, I know what you are thinking, the resemblance betwixt my brother and me is such that we could be twins." Here, Mateo stopped and laughed at his own jest, before continuing. "Tis true we were not birthed of the same mother, but we are *Family* none the less. If you would allow us the honor, we would be more than willing to escort you to the Land Duck Inn as it is merely a short walk away." As he finished, Mateo gestured towards the open door.

"I think that would be a good idea," said Ferika who followed Mel out of the door. Once outside, Mateo walked on the opposite side of her than his brother. Ferika noted that both men took special care not to get too close to her. She also spotted several of the merchants in the area (particularly the women) giving the men furtive glances of thanks, while others seemed too ashamed of their inaction to look upon the trio.

As they walked, the brothers took turns talking to Ferika. They pointed out various localities of note, such as where one could go to acquire weapons and armor of the finest quality, which general store offered the best wares and which establishments were best to be avoided. Their description of the Sunder's Dawn Menagerie, a collection of exotic animals, run by an enterprising female gnome by the name of Dabenog Taukabbo was particularly engaging since it was Mateo's favorite attraction in the whole town.

While the brothers did not spend much time talking about themselves, they did fill Ferika in on some of the dangers of the city. They explained that there were three main gangs vying for control of Sunder's Dawn's streets. The largest of the gangs was the X Town Growlers, a group that focused mainly on prostitution and the sale of illicit drugs, including the highly addictive Star Dust. The X Town Growlers are extremely proud of themselves and hate the term Xrs, which many call them behind their back, but very few would dare say to their face. The Xrs Ferika had the altercation with were young initiates who knew their bark was much more than their bite. Had some of the more senior members been around, then the brothers might have had to prove their words with action.

The second biggest gang was the Demon Dogs. They were known primarily for small time corruption schemes and protection shakedowns. They are a constant nuisance in the town but have paid off many members of law enforcement and thus have little to fear from authorities.

The third, and in Mel's estimation, the most dangerous of the three gangs is the Maniacs. The Maniacs excel at creating fear through public beatings, torture, or even death. Every member of the Maniacs is said to be a heartless killer. Occasionally they hire on as mercenaries to gain more skill and increase the notoriety of their gang. Maniacs can be identified by a teardrop tattoo under their left eye that they get after their initiation, which includes the death of some unfortunate wretch.

"And on that cheery note, you have arrived at your destination." quipped Mateo as they rounded a corner and headed towards a sprawling two-story structure with rich architecture and an elegantly crafted marvel sign of a duck, with ducklings in tow, ambling across a field of tall grass. The words Land Duck were carved beneath the duck's feet.

Mel opened the door for Ferika and Mateo. It took Ferika's eyes a moment to adjust as the light within was much dimmer than outside. As she scanned the area, she could see they were in an opulently appointed waiting area of sorts. The large circular entrance had a single cushioned bench built into the right-hand wall. On the left side, there was a massive oak front desk, behind which stood a well-dressed young lady and with servants waiting to assist customers with any luggage. A large set of glass double doors separated the waiting room from the rest of the inn.

The two men waited to the side as Ferika walked towards the desk. However, before she had crossed the distance, one of the glass doors opened up and a large female stepped out to greet her. "Feri? Is that you?" asked the eight-foot three-inch elon female whose smile was broad and warm. "By the spirits, you have grown into such a lovely young woman. A little skinny perhaps, I mean, I can't see you swinging that sword for hours on end, but what could you expect from them Alms."

The sound of that booming voice, and the sight of the massive warrior, brought relief and instant cheer to Ferika's heart and the teen rushed over and buried herself within Ivara's warm embrace. It had been nearly four years since they last saw each other, but Ferika felt as if Ivara was ever with her.

"You have no idea how good it is to see you!" Ferika stated after extricating herself from her friend's clutches. "The road from Kelitan was long and trying and then I had a run in with some of these Xr boys that would have ended very badly if it weren't for these two here." Ferika ended as she turned to gesture towards the brothers who were approaching the pair. It did not escape Ferika's notice that the attendants were listening intently to their conversation and shared sad but knowing looks at her mention of the Xrs.

"Run in with the Xrs huh? And these guys came to save the day?" queried the large brown skinned woman, whose curly hair was pulled back into a bushy bun. Ferika nearly laughed as the elon's protective nature took over and she interposed herself between the two men and her young friend. Addressing Mateo and Mel, the elon said, "I am Ivara Stonegrinder, long-time friend of the little one here, and you are?"

"Infatuated by your beauty," answered Mel without a moment's hesitation. His eyes were filled with honest adoration as he gazed up at Ivara's beautiful face. As an elon, Ivara looked like a regular human female except for her great height and the fact that all elons possessed athletically built physiques. Ivara's arms, and what little of her legs that were exposed, were lean with muscle and spoke to her great potential as a fighter.

"Apologies my lady, what my smitten brother meant to say is that his name is Mel Uhneen and mine is Mateo La'ahtyne. We are pleased to have been so fortunate as to have the opportunity to offer this fair lady some assistance in her time of need." He finished by sketching a courtly bow that had Mel rolling his eyes in amusement.

"Well, my thanks to you both, but I feel there is a tale here that needs to be told," Ivara began as she gestured towards the glass doors. "My friend and I were just sitting down to enjoy a meal. I would be pleased if you would join us to tell us more of today's events."

From the causal way in which she dismissed their flattering words, Mel could tell it was not the first time she had heard such. *Okay, business first and hopefully romance later,* he thought. But to the group he said, "Thanks for the gracious offer. We will happily provide any information that you would like."

The first thing Ferika noticed when they walked through the double doors was the savory smell coming from the inn's kitchen. Following that, she found herself impressed with the opulence of the establishment. The oak floor was partially covered by a thick carpet decorated with warm colors arranged in a geometric pattern. Two thirds of the room was filled with sturdy round tables and cushioned chairs. The other side of the room held a large bar of polished wood behind which stood a wide selection of beverages in fancy bottles. Separating the bar from the eating area was an open space where several customers were dancing to a little ditty played by a female halfling on a small, raised stage. Two stairways rested at the opposite ends of the room. Both provided access to the upper level, while the one closest to the bar also had stairs that went down. The room reminded her of some of the grand feast halls maintained by a few Jarls that ruled over wealthy Keltan clans in her homeland up north.

Standing up from one of the tables was a strapping soaren dwarf that stood a little over four feet tall. The approaching dwarf had kind eyes, light brown skin and long black hair that was pulled back into two thick corn rows. The dwarf's wings were folded smoothly over his broad shoulders and appeared very much like a cloak with colors of white and several different shades of brown. The dwarf beamed an easy smile as he scooped the taller human up in an embrace.

"Ah little Feri, it has been too long," the dwarf said after gently placing the elated teen back on solid ground. "I can't wait to hear all the tales you have from your time in the Norrilands" he added, referring to the forest territory controlled by the Kelitan people.

"I didn't know you'd be bringing friends along. The name is Grimlocke Direstroke, but my friends call me Grim. Glad to meet you fellows," the dwarf spoke as he stepped up and extended his forearm to the brothers. After clasping forearms with each of the brothers, Grim added "Any friend of Feri's is a friend of mine."

"Grim, you haven't changed a bit," said Ferika as she reached out to hold the dwarf's hand. "These two didn't travel with me. In fact, I just met them a short while ago. This is Mel and Mateo."

"It appears our young friend had a run in with some thugs earlier." Ivara stated as she indicated everyone should take a seat at their table. "These two intervened and I was hoping to learn more over a meal." Grim could see Ivara's eye-teeth were slightly more elongated than usual. That coupled with a thickening of her nails indicated she was becoming agitated. Thanks to her elon heritage, Ivara's genetics altered based on outside stimuli. The four years she had lived with a werewolf clan had caused her to adapt as a feran, which heightened her fighting prowess and other senses. Seeing the affect the news was having on his young friend, Grim was determined to capture every detail of the story told by Ferika and the two brothers.

About an hour later, after the meal of smoked pheasant, baked potatoes slathered in a savory mushroom sauce, and heavily peppered diced-carrots and onions, Grim sat digesting the information he had just learned. While he was familiar with the gangs of Sunder's Dawn, he had never had an altercation with them before. To be honest, he and his companions didn't frequent this town very much. Their occupation as treasure hunters took them to many different areas, and he had only been in Sunder's Dawn about three times in the past few years.

For a time, everyone was silent as the serving lad scooped up their plates and refreshed their glasses. Ivara broke the silence as she looked at Grim and said, "You know what has to be done. We can't let them get away with that. I mean, just imagine what would have happened."

"But I'm okay," Ferika said, feeling a growing unease at the thought of hunting down those men. "Mel seemed to know one of them," she continued in almost a pleading voice. "Maybe we can just report this to the authorities and let them handle it."

"I wish it were that easy," retorted Mel as he and Mateo shared knowing glances. "Recall what I was telling you about impunity. The Xrs have many of the authorities in their pocket. I would be surprised if they even made a perfunctory show of investigating the matter. More likely, they would try to find a way to make it out to be your fault. It seems to me if justice is to be had, it will be at the edge of a sword rather than by the dictates of the law."

"Now Feri," Grim began, his voice full of compassion as he turned to gaze at her directly. "I know you are studying to become a member of the Society of Alms. I think that is admirable and agree with the society's goal of spreading peace and healing, but in this situation, I am in total agreement with Ivara." Ferika didn't miss the shocked look on Ivara' face, as she shared the same feeling. Grim was often the one that cautioned against making rash decisions. His inclination was to talk matters out, rather than resorting to violence. Seeing her reaction, the dwarf gave a sad smile, then said, "Think it through. Some people are just bad and need to be put down. Imagine how you will feel if you learn that tomorrow they grabbed another young girl who wasn't able to get away? Besides, Falzadrin is one of my oldest friends. I can't let something like this happen to his kin and not be addressed."

"I guess… I mean, I know you're right. I just hate the whole situation." Ferika said as her shoulders slumped in defeat. "It's probably a mute, point anyway since I doubt, we'll be able to find them." Her tone made it clear that she was grasping at straws with the possibility that their prey might elude them.

"Well, in truth, I that you will not have far to look," said Mateo as he downed the last of his cherry fusion. "You see, the Xrs had one of their spotters tailing us from the market. He is a scrawny lad with disheveled black hair, a gray cowl, and brown pants. As we stepped into the Land Duck Inn, he ducked into the alley across the way. I am sure he is waiting for you to leave, so that his fellows can finish what they started earlier."

Ivara and Grim exchanged looks of determination as Mateo continued. "My hermano and I were going to see to this matter, but since you have capable allies and we have pressing matters of our own to contend with, we will leave this in your capable hands." With that Mateo stood, dropped a few silvers on the table and bowed to the companions.

Before saying his farewells, Mel offered a warning to the group. "While I have no doubt you will win the day, you must know that you will be marked for your actions. If I were you, I would make plans to leave this place post-haste once the deed is done. In this town, the reach of the Xrs is long and you may not be safe thereafter."

Hours later, Grimlocke alighted on the balcony outside of the room that Ivara and Ferika shared. He entered the door to the suite and shut the curtains as he closed the door. The two women were sitting on their respective beds, attempting to gain a little rest, while waiting for his return. Grimlocke could sense Ivara's eagerness as she practically leapt up upon his entrance. Conversely, Ferika looked as if this evening's outing was the last thing she would rather do. Part of Grimlocke sympathized with the teen as he understood violence was not the preferred path of the peace-loving Society of Alms, and that Ferika has bought in to that line fully.

However, the reality of EverLore was such that violence was a fact of life, and sometimes was the last resort of the downtrodden. *The sooner that Ferika internalized this lesson, the better*, Grim thought as he took out his magnificent dwarven cleaver (a wide bladed weapon of dwarven design that was a cross between a sword and an ax).

"The spotter is still outside, and it appears he has been joined by another Xr." Grimlocke began as the two women stood up and began securing their weapons and other items. "I have already prepared the horses and pack mule. They are tied up outside of Faldrin's Anvil."

"So, we're really doing this?" asked Ferika, her voice dripping with nervous apprehension. As a Keltan, Ferika had received martial training from an early age. Her people were considered to be very warlike and frequently launched raids on far away locales seeking slaves or riches. Ferika had even been forced to go on one such raid, but that was nearly four years ago, and her main task during the time was to care for the warrior's equipment and prepare the food. Following that, she petitioned her jarl (the leader of her clan) to be allowed to join the Society of Alms. Ferika was no fan of violence and thought tonight's actions were misguided. However, she trusted Grim and Ivara and just wanted to get this over as soon as possible.

"Yes," answered Grimlocke. "Just follow the plan as we discussed. Wait a few minutes after I leave before heading out. Once clear of the Land Duck Inn, make a beeline directly for Faldrin's Anvil. It'll take a bit of time for Faldrin to ensure Ivara's new gear fits correctly. That should give our eager friends a chance to set up their ambush. If all goes well, I should be able to locate them and inform Ivara so you guys are ready when you exit."

Putting a comforting arm around Ferika, Ivara's tone was gentle as she said, "Look Feri, I know your heart isn't in this, but your mind needs to be. When the fighting starts, I'll try to protect you as much as I am able, but I need to know you will be ready to fend off any threats that may come your way."

"I know what I have to do," Ferika stated flatly, while focusing her mind on the many hours of combat training she'd had.

"Well, I guess we better get this thing going," responded Grimlocke as he moved to the door. "Make sure you pay for our stay on your way out. I am not sure when, or if, we'll be by this way again."

Before opening the door, Grimlocke cast a knowing glance at Ivara and quipped, "Do try to keep your emotions in check, at least until the fighting starts." Grimlocke had to make a quick exit to avoid the mock kick sent his way by the young elon. The Xrs are in for a world of hurt when that one gets her claws on them, Grimlocke thought as he took flight and began making, what appeared to be a casual circuit of the town.

"Time for the hunt," Grimlocke spoke into the air, confident that his enchanted earring would send the message to its twin on Ivara's left ear. "Looks like there are three of them Xrs down there now. I'll keep a watch until you two are out and then make my way to a good lookout spot near Faldrin's place."

Twenty minutes later, Ivara and Ferika were walking down the streets of Sunder's Dawn. The sky was still bright with daylight, but hints of shadow on the horizon heralded the coming arrival of evening hues. The atmosphere was quite lively as townsfolk scurried from place to place, living their own lives without a clue of the deadly cat and mouse game that was playing out right before their eyes.

As they wound through the streets, headed for Faldrin's Anvil, Ivara kept up a steady conversation, designed to put Feri at ease, as well as throw off any potential eavesdroppers. Although Ivara was looking forward to the coming confrontation, she was not foolhardy enough to believe it came without the possibility of peril. She took comfort in

Grim's routine updates.

Turning onto Hemlock Road, Ivara could see the solid stone structure of Faldrin's Anvil, tucked between two larger establishments. The streets were not as crowded in this district, as many of the shops were assisting the last of the night's customers while preparing to close up for the night. Strolling down the covered porch, that connected all of the buildings on this side of the road, Ivara was surprised to see an elf step out of Faldrin's Anvil.

"Well, you don't see that every day," Ivara said to Ferika as she motioned toward the elf, who was walking towards the alley that separated Faldrin's Anvil from Rook's Clothier, an apparel shop that catered to the more affluent citizens of Sunder's Dawn. The elf was just rounding the corner as a well-dressed man came out of the same alley. The man sneered and spat at the elf's feet before shouting, "Stinking elf, go back and hide in the dank trees where you belong!" The elf looked as if he were about to take some type of action, when his burvore companion placed a hand on his arm and pulled him hastily into the alley.

The man let out a self-congratulatory laugh and gave the woman a suggestive wink as he started to walk past them. Without breaking stride, Ivara casually shoved the man off of the walkway, and sent him sprawling into the street, muddying his fine garments. Her actions irritated the horses and pack mule that were tied outside of Faldrin's Anvil, and caused more than a few of the town's people to look her way and laugh as the man floundered to his feet.

"Apologies for your rudeness," Ivara scoffed as she held the door open for Ferika to enter. Before letting the door close behind her, Ivara gave the man a scathing look, as if daring him to say something. Wisely, he did not, and so she turned to the establishment's patron and gave the man no further thought.

"Well now, that was quite entertaining," said Faldrin as he came to clasp forearms with the tall elon. Faldrin's light brown skin was crisscrossed with many scars, and his light brown eyes seemed alight with a fire stolen from the very forge by which he made his living. "I didn't know you were so fond of elves," he finished as he took a last look out to see the man pull himself off the street, before walking away with his head held low.

"I got no love for elves, but even they deserve to be treated with some modicum of respect. I really should have let the matter go, but then what lesson would that have sent?" Ferika knew Ivara's question was aimed at her like an arrow and could not deflect the sting of its blow. "Noted," she said letting a bit of her frustration seep into her words. Elves were an unfortunate creation of Danu (Goddess of Nature). They lived pathetic little lives within their forest homes, thinking themselves superior to other races. While Ferika had never had any personal dealings with elves she had heard stories of them double crossing traders, harassing and robbing travelers, and committing all kinds of atrocities to peaceful wonderers of the woods. Though she would not say it outwardly, especially not in Ivara's presence, the young Keltan tended to agree that elves should stick with their own kind.

In the ensuing silence, Ferika glanced around the spacious storefront. As with any other smithies, the walls of Faldrin's Anvil were lined with a wide assortment of weapons and other gear favored by adventurers. However, what drew her attention were the fanciful glass cases that were stationed around the room. Each of the six cases housed a splendid suit of polished armor. Ferika didn't have to open herself up to the Shadow Sea to be able to feel the strong magical energy that flowed from a few of the wondrous items.

"I'm assuming you're here to pick up your armor," said Faldrin as the silence extended to the point of discomfort. "My husband put the finishing touches on it just this morning, and will be happy to ensure it fits well and is repaired according to your standards." With that, he gestured to the dwarf that had come from behind the counter and was approaching the group.

"It's good to see you again Trovkil," Ivara said as she clasped forearms with the dwarf. The dwarf's pale skin stood out in stark contrast with the deep brown of Ivara's own.

"And you as well, my lady," Trovkil responded as he ushered Ivara over to the dressing halls situated behind a heavy partitioning curtain. He then went to bring her armor from the back workroom.

Faldrin introduced himself to Ferika, and then struck up a conversation with her as they waited for Ivara and Trovkil to return. Ferika was glad to speak with the friendly dwarf, if for no other reason than it distracted her from the unpleasantness that awaited outside. Yet, the young human found herself genuinely engaged as the dwarf recounted how he and his husband came to run this establishment. Ferika heard the words of her own father, as Faldrin discussed his hope and concerns over the future of his adopted daughter, Sherkzin, who was learning the family trade and would one day inherit this shop and more.

Ferika was more than a little disappointed when at last Ivara stepped from behind the curtain, wearing her restored armored long coat. The brown leather overcoat, appeared similar to a regular garment, but contained strategically placed metal plates to add protection for the wearer.

She watched in silence as Ivara paid her bill for the repairs. The elon turned towards Ferika and allowed her eyes to wander, as she listened to a final update from the watching Grimlocke.

"Feri, it's time," she said, placing her hands on the girl's shoulders. "Get that stick of yours out and get ready to make it dance."

She began walking to the door, as Ferika fell in line behind her. "Fellas, there's gonna be quite a ruckus outside. I know your hearts, and ask that you two do not involve yourselves. There is bound to be some blow back from what we are about to do, and I would hate for any of it to fall onto you. I'm afraid we're about to make a right mess of some of them Xr boys."

"I hear you lass, and thank ye for your concern. But if things look to go bad for yourself and your little friend there, know that my ax will soon be wet with the blood of the X," answered Faldrin as he stepped behind the counter and placed a hand on the ax resting there.

"There is a hammer in the back that I have been dying to test out," spoke Trovkil as he started for the back room, "But this might also help sway The Luck to smile on you," he added.

Ivara felt the familiar tingle as a spell of protection dropped over her and, she assumed, Feri. The reference to Vanidor (the God of Adventure) who was often referred to as The Luck, always seemed to smile on her in matters of combat.

"Many thanks," she called back as she stepped out into the street just to see a body fall from the heavens to crush a burly figure standing within a ring of warriors.

Darkness had descended upon Sunder's Dawn as Grimlocke made his final aerial circuit of Hemlock Road. He had identified three snipers on various rooftops around Faldrin's Anvil. Two of the men had crossbows and a third held a wand and casually leaned against the side of a chimney as he waited for the action to begin. On ground level, Grimlocke could make out thirteen men, that had set up a semi-circular perimeter around the front of Faldrin's shop, well situated to cut off any avenues of escape for their perceived prey.

As Ivara had surmised, the Xrs didn't appear to have associated his coming and goings with the two women, because he had yet to see any of them so much as glance to the sky. Not that it would have mattered, other than the Xr with the wand, Grimlocke was sure the magic of his *Concealment* spell would have hidden him from most prying eyes. Down below, a woman exited Rook's Clothier carrying a rug and a paddle-like stick. She held the rug aloft in one hand and began beating it with the other hand. The dust from the paddle hitting the rug fell onto the street, and the rhythmic noise of the cleansing gave Grimlocke the perfect opportunity to strike.

When he was around ten feet above the lounging wandsman, Grimlocke silently pulled out his dwarven cleaver. He then collapsed his wings and fell to the rooftop, slashing his cleaver across the face of the unsuspecting foe. Grimlocke skimmed the other rooftops to see if he had been discovered and was happy to note the other two snipers had their attention focused squarely on the road below. Any sound of his attack was drowned out by the woman below, who was just then finishing and starting to head back in to the shop. Putting away his dwarven cleaver, Grimlocke reached out his left arm and a mighty longbow appeared in his waiting hands.

Grimlocke took a breath to center himself, before opening himself up to the great flow of the Shadow Sea. He quickly located the path that he sought and redirected the currents to create a Portal Breach spell. Once that was complete, Grimlocke edged around the chimney stack until he had a direct line of sight on one of the rooftop snipers. After the barest of hesitations, he let loose an arrow that leapt across the distance to bury itself in his target's neck. Even as his victim clutched the mortal wound and fell back onto the roof, Grimlocke released his grip on the bow, and stepped into the waiting portal.

The third sniper was just responding to the actions of his fellow attacker when Grimlocke stepped out of the portal and stabbed him though the back with wing tips that hardened into sharpened spears. The impaled man gurgled blood as Grimlocke pulled him close and snapped his neck.

"It's showtime," Grimlocke whispered, as the enchanted tattoo on his arm glowed a soft blue due to the magic of the dissolving bow returned unto it. With barely an effort, Grimlocke grabbed the dead man and launched into the air. He then released the man to fall on the ring leader of the Xrs assembled below.

The sound of bones crunching and meat hitting the ground was soon joined by the startled cry of several of the Xrs as Ivara burst onto the street with a feral snarl of rage exiting her throat. Within two mighty strides, she sank her elongated claws into the throat of the first Xr in her path and tore out his adam's apple as she tossed him aside like a broken rag doll. A laugh escaped her lips as she flung the bloody morsal at a second man, before leaping into the air to plant her knee into the face of a muscle-bound orceen nearly as tall as she. The would-be assailant's face exploded beneath the force of the attack and Ivara road his corpse to the ground before executing a front roll that had her coming up to face a fourth man that soon found himself being hurled at the fifth in line.

Overcome by the savagery of Ivara's attack, Ferika stood frozen in place. She had seen warriors of her people fall into a berserker rage when in the throes of battle, but never before had she been so close to someone that fought with such ferocity. Ferika's distraction nearly cost her life as the blade of an Xr came speeding in, to bounce off a magical shield that sent sparks flying into the air. Only then, did the girl remember herself and set her quarterstaff in line to deflect the second blow.

Retreating a few steps, Ferika allowed her attacker to take the initiative. Her mind worked to fall into rhythm with the man as she blocked each of his thrusts and finally countered with a strike intended for his temple. However, the man reacted faster than she anticipated and pulled up short, allowing the staff to sail past before aiming a strike at her midsection. Without thinking, Ferika dropped her staff and allowed her body to fall back, like a reed in the wind. Time seemed to slow as she saw the blade pass overhead. As soon as her back hit the ground, Ferika rolled her legs over her head and rapidly flung them back towards her enemy. She used the momentum of her descending legs to fling her shoulders into the air and soon stood facing the unbalanced attacker. She kicked her right foot into the man's left knee, with enough force to hear a crack. Seeing the man fall, Ferika rushed out to pick up her wayward staff.

One of the Xrs threw up his hands in her direction and Ferika's whole body simply froze up as magic washed over her. The man then leaped into the air as wings of pure energy sprouted from his back and hurled him towards the descending soaren dwarf. However, the mages trajectory swiftly changed as a leaping Ivara, shouting, "Get down here," crashed into him and causing them both to smash through a window on the other side of the street.

Assured that Ivara could handle the mage, Grimlocke landed, placing himself between the paralyzed Ferika and four advancing Xrs. When the men were no more than fifteen feet away, Grimlocke flexed his wings sending a shower of hardened feathers to buffet the enemy. He then closed the distance, lifting his shield to deflect the first blow of a scrawny looking human before raking his blade along the man's arm, slicing tendons and rendering it useless. As the man fell, Grimlocke bashed the flat of his shield into the face of the man's comrade, earning a spout of blood for his effort.

"Ah, by Bran's bronze beard," shouted Grimlocke as pain lanced his side from a spear thrust of one of the Xrs, that had thus far escaped his notice.

"The Protector God won't be helping you today," called the spearman as his weapon descended for another strike.

"Maybe not, but I will," yelled Ferika as she frantically worked to perry the spear thrust with her staff. She then took a wild swing at the spearman, that wasn't truly meant to connect. Instead, it served to distract him so that he was ill prepared when a flying head, tossed out of the nearby store window, smacked into the side of his face. Ferika took advantage of her opponent's predicament by stepping forward and jabbing her staff directly into his exposed throat.

Stepping out of the broken window, Ivara raised the headless corpse into the air using only one hand, before issuing a roar more suited for some dark forest than a town street. Somewhere in the back of her mind, Ivara registered an answering roar, just before seeing three men bolt out of the alleyway beside Faldrin's Anvil, but her blood was up and these things instantly fell from her thoughts. The rage in Ivara's eyes, the blood dripping from her fang filled mouth, and the fact that she was even then turning their way, caused the remaining Xrs to turn tail and flee for their lives. Even still, one of them was clipped from behind as Ivara hurled the corpse at him. Before the man could get up, Ivara was there and rammed her foot into his back, sending him back into the dirt of the road. She reached around and pulled out the dagger on the man's belt and then proceeded to cut the outline of an eye in his back.

Once done, Ivara tossed the weapon aside and turned to those brave, or stupid enough, to sit around as onlookers and said in Wood Tongue, "Let it be known that from this day forth, the actions of the Xrs and others will not go unpunished. You may think to get away with what is done in the dark, but you won't. For we are always watching."

With one last look at the carnage they had wrought, Ivara climbed onto the horse that was brought over by Grimlocke, before riding away. As she left, Lorat extracted himself from the body he was under and stood up. His blonde hair was slick with dirt and blood and the pain of his back was neigh unbearable. Anger, fear and embarrassment warred within him. He was embarrassed by the lack of respect he saw in the eyes of those who had witnessed this fiasco. He was angered by the thought that some whore could do this to him in his own town. But deep down, Lorat knew fear the most; fear of the savage beast that had so casually slaughtered so many of the guys he grew up with. Stumbling from the scene of his eternal shame, Lorat made his way back to one of the X Town Growler's safe houses. There he told his tale and waited for it to reach the ears of the leader of the gang, the dread warrior once called Losaginus X, but now who insisted on being referred to only as He Who Is They.

Chapter 4:
Sunder's Dawn

The sounds of birds chirping, the trickling of water in the nearby pond, and other noises of the early spring morning slowly began to worm their way into Niska's dreams. However, it was the sultry smell of fried bacon, eggs and warmed bread that brought her fully awake. She rolled out of her sleeping bag and stood up, stretching life back into her muscles. Z'har sat across from the fire, scooping food out of the black steel pan and putting it on the two wooden plates they had with them. From the sheen of sweat that hung across his brow, Niska surmised he had been up for an hour or two, most likely running himself through rigorous martial practice.

"Another dream then," Niska asked as she sat down beside him and accepted the plate from her friend. Her eyes held the concern that weighed heavily on her heart. Z'har was not sleeping well over the last few months, and the lack of sleep was showing in his frayed nerves and growing temper.

"More of the same," Z'har sighed as a yawn escaped his open mouth. "She's there, and I'm there, both her rescuer and her murderer. I've tried everything I can think of to make sense of the things she says, but nothing works. I can only comprehend a few phrases. The rest is… muddled somehow." The weariness in Z'har's voice matched the bags below his youthful eyes. He took several healthy bites of his food, before continuing, "I know I need to find her, but I'm starting to think that she will be better off if I don't."

Setting her plate aside, Niska scooted closer to Z'har and put her arm around him, "I understand your concerns, but we've been through this before. Believe me, you're not some mindless killer. There's a mystery surrounding this young half-elf that we have yet to ferret out. When the time comes that we find her, things will work out." Niska used her free hand to gently tug on Z'har's braided hair, coaxing him to look down at her. When she had his full attention, she continued, "When that time comes… whatever happens, we'll face it together."

"I know," answered Z'har as he gave her a slight nod and mustered a weak smile. "Now finish your food, so we can get going. I thought you were going to sleep the whole day away."

After eating, Niska went down and washed herself in the stream. Upon return, she took over packing up their things and encouraged Z'har to go do the same. This was the first opportunity they'd had to spend a peaceful morning and cleanse their body, and mind, in at least a tenday. She knew that the simple act of falling back into old routines would help sooth Z'har's troubled soul.

As she watched the elf walk towards the stream, Niska's mind strolled along the paths of their month's long journey from Skyfall. While it had been cold, their journey within the Valley of Shale had not been an unpleasant one. They were familiar with much of the terrain and even managed to stop in and visit with a few families they knew along the way.

When they got to the Havershorn Caves, a mazelike network of caverns that runs beneath the Eversoar Mountains and connect the Palen Wood to the Archstone Range, they awaited the arrival of the Mensra'Adul (the Keepers of the Gate). Neither of the two had any previous encounters with the Mensra'Adul, but knew enough to treat these strange beings with the utmost respect. Even now, Niska's mind was fuzzy as she tried to focus on details of the Mensra'Adul members that she had traveled. She remembered them being humanoid, some had the semblance of dwarves, while others simulated the features of other races. Over the next tenday, as the Mensra'Adul led them under the Eversoar Mountains, Niska's zin nature allowed her to pierce the facade of these creatures and catch a glimpse of their true forms. What she saw, she did not fully understand as they seemed to exist in dual realities, always in flux, with bodies that merged with the rock and air around them. Whatever they were, Niska was sure their origins were extraplanar. The tenor of their journey changed when they reached the Archstone Range.

"Asleep on the job, I see," called Z'har, jarring Niska from her memories and causing her to realize how little packing she had actually been doing.

"Apologies, slave driver," Niska said with mirth, "I just thought I'd leave a bit for you to take care of."

As she and Z'har struck camp, carefully doused the fire, and prepared to set off, Niska smiled to herself because she could see a bounce in Z'har's steps and an ease in his shoulders that hadn't been there for some time. She determined to continue to find ways to help coax him out of his malaise and to prepare him for whatever dangers they were walking into.

More than six hours later, Niska and Z'har stood upon the rise of a grass covered hill, looking down at the town of Sunder's Dawn. From their vantage point, they could see much of the town' layout. The burvore noted that Z'har appeared to be scanning the town's walls with interest.

"Up and over, do you think?" she asked Z'har after a time.

"That was my initial thought," answered Z'har without taking his eyes from the city. "I can see that they're working on beefing up the walls, but they still remain a pale comparison to those surrounding the keeps of Skyfall. I don't think it would take much work at all to scale those timbers. Plus, their guard stations appear to be way too far apart. If we wait until nightfall, it would make it that much easier."

"So why do I hear hesitation in your voice?" Niska responded, as her thoughts had run pretty much along the same track.

"I was just thinking to myself that it somehow feels too easy," Z'har stated after a moment. "I'm guessing the town planners realized the same thing we did, and probably have some magical deterrent in place to compensate for the inadequacy of the wall. My guess is they have several trap-spells to hinder the progress of any would-be assailants. With the way the people of the Archstone range have responded to me thus far, I can't imagine I would receive a warm welcome if we were caught scaling the walls."

Niska watched as sad resignation descended upon

Z'har's handsome face. "I take your point," she intoned, and then patted the sack on her hip with a mischievous grin. Her smile grew even larger, as Z'har caught on to her meaning and gave an exasperated sigh. "Yup, it looks like the sack-trick once again."

"May the spirits take you and your blasted splinter sac," retorted Z'har as he contemplated once again spending time within the dimensional space created by the enchanted bag. Being within the splinter sac really wasn't all that bad. Z'har and Niska had used this method several times before when seeking to ferret one or the other into places where they were not supposed to be. In fact, he kind of enjoyed it. It provided a quiet place of solitude where meditation came easy. The only thing was, whenever he was within the magically created dimension, his mind would always run to the worst-case scenario where something would happen to Niska and he would be trapped in there until he eventually starved to death.

"Don't worry, old man, I'll toss some food in with you this time.," Niska giggled, knowing exactly what thoughts were running through Z'har's mind. "Look there," Niska said in a more serious tone, while pointing down to the stream of visitors that were lined up outside the town. "I'll slip in with them, and get you out as soon as it is clear. I should have no problem remaining undetected, and hopefully we can avoid any of the unpleasantness from the last few stops."

There was no need to elaborate on that last bit as she recalled how the guards of Onsterwall, the first settlement in the Archstone range they encountered upon exiting the Valley of Shale, had outright refused to let an elf pass through their gates. The reception wasn't much better at Budenholt, the next community in line. They only allowed Z'har in after assigning two of the village guard to accompany him and monitor his every move. This had irked Niska and Z'har, but their options were limited as their supplies had run low and they needed to restock. Worst still was the reaction of the Krozites. There, Z'har was the butt of many rude remarks and accusations and the pair were forced to defend themselves when five men thought it was their right to "put the demon-spawned pointy-ear in his place." That did not end well for the men, but accumulation of all of the injustice was wearing on them both.

"Well, let's get this over with," said Z'har as he motioned towards the splinter sac. Niska removed the enchanted sac from her hip and held it open. As soon as Z'har placed his hand within it, Niska willed the internal space to accept him, and watched as he was instantly transported within. She then secured the sac once again on her belt and headed down the hill towards Sunder's Dawn.

The sun was riding high in the sky as Niska insinuated herself into the line of people headed for the town. Most were human or dwarven, but a scattering of dreks, shakarans and other races could also be found. She wound her way through the crowd and was happy to see that most were engaged in lively conversations and barely paid her any mind. That was just as well, she thought as she passed a group of humans with several small kids in tow and positioned herself beside a wagon being pulled by two large oxen. Niska walked along with the wagon for several paces gaging its speed and the rotation of its wheels to ensure that her timing would be right. She casually looked around, ensuring no one was watching her before rolling under the wagon, deftly slipping between its two right-side wheels. Once beneath the wagon, she used her sharp claws to dig into its underbelly and pull herself from the ground.

"Mammah, did you see that badger thing get crushed by that..." began a small boy in the group behind the wagon before he was interrupted by his mother who gave him a solid slap on the back of his head and angrily said, "Hush up now boy, didn't I tell you never to interrupt when grown folks is talkin!"

"But, I..." the boy started to protest, before shutting his mouth and flinching away from another threatened blow.

Sorry, kid, Niska thought to herself as she let her muscles ease into their old pattern. She had practiced this maneuver many times back in Skyfall. All of the Fallowsheirs had trained long and hard in the art of combat, but a select few also gained training in the art of infiltration and information gathering. Niska reckoned that she could perhaps hold this position for about thirty minutes, but was not looking forward to testing that theory. Luckily for her, just a short twelve minutes later the cart pulled to a halt as a female voice range out "Buntok, it has been too long. I thought one of them wild creatures had surely put an end to you."

"Nah, Tazawnya, you should know by now that my old hide is too tough for any of them mangy mutts to take a proper bite out of," laughed the half orc, his mouth opening wide to reveal the full length of his tusks. Buntok took more after his orc mother than his human father and was quite sturdy, with meaty limbs, a pronounced jaw, and pale, yellow eyes. "I did get me a young azirian hound. Ounce she calms down and grows a bit, she should make a right enough mate for Uftoff. That one's been lonely ever since Hribxus died nearly a year back. Got some other critters back there along with her. You can take a peek if you like, just be careful and mind the hound's tail."

"A new azirian, you say!" responded the guard excitedly as she stepped around to the side of the wagon. "This, I've got to see!"

Niska saw the legs of the guard move to the rear of the wagon, and then heard the rustling of fabric as the guard pulled aside a portion of the wagon's covering. The sound of frantic shuffling could be heard from the creatures within the cart's many cages. Oohs and aahs echoed from the crowd as many of those in line scrambled closer to get a better view. Just then, a low growl could be heard as something banged against the side of one of the enclosures. Niska could picture the large hound (perhaps four or five feet at the shoulders, if still a pup) showing its double rows of fangs as it banged against the cage and lashed out at the crowd, attempting to maim a careless observer with the barb hidden in the fur of its tail.

"Whoa now!" shouted Buntok as he cast a glance towards the back of the cart. "Calm down girl," he continued, speaking to the azirian hound in a soothing voice. He then stood in the wagon seat and opened his arms wide to address the gathering crowd. "I know you lot are just itchin for a show. Fear not, you can see all of these little beauties and many more, at the Sunder's Dawn Menagerie. In fact, when you get there, just tell em that Buntok the Beautiful sent ye and I'm sure they'll be reducing the price of entry. But fer now, the show is over, and I must be getting on me way."

The big orceen was grinning ear to ear by the time Tazawnya, who had carefully replaced the tarp, stepped back around to his side. "If I didn't know any better, I'd say you just used me to advertise the town's zoo," she giggled.

Touching his index finger to the tip of his nose, Buntok did not reply, but his eyes said indeed he had.

"Get on with ye, you old dog," Tazawnya said as she playfully slapped the orceen's leg. She knew that Dabenog Taukabbo, the menagerie's owner would be pleased with Buntok's craftiness.

Niska heard the orceen reply, "Always a pleasure, my dear," as the cart lurched into motion, causing her to flex her tense muscles in order to maintain her purchase. The world rolled by upside down as she watched them pass the walls and weave their way into the crowd of wagons, horses and pedestrians traversing the town's streets.

Niska's muscles began screaming at her several minutes later and she knew it was time to extract herself from this topsy-turvy world. Summoning her zin ability (the innate power residing within her), the burvore caused a stump of gravel and dirt to spring up beneath a food stand several strides to her wagon's left. The stump lifted the stand enough to tip it over, and then dissolved according to Niska's will. The sly burvore used the ensuing confusion to scramble from under the wagon and lose herself in the crowd.

Niska walked around the town a bit, letting the ache bleed from her muscles and regaining more of her natural vigor. The smells of savory food tickled at her nostrils, forcing Niska to admit how hungry she was. She and Z'har had stocked plenty of provisions for their trip, but the road was longer than they expected and their trail rations were running quite low. She followed her nose for a few blocks and eventually wound up in a large open-air market. *Perfect*, she thought to herself, *I can learn how to find Faldrin's Anvil and get a proper meal all in one place.*

The sun was still high overhead and the air was crisp and clean. The market, which she later learned was called the Starbright Market, was abuzz with people and activity.

Niska had to make a stop at four different vendor stalls before being provided directions to Faldrin's Anvil. It wasn't that the other vendors didn't know where the shop was. It was that they said they could only provide information to paying customers, and since their stalls didn't have anything she wanted, she was encouraged to move along. Luckily, a dwarven merchant named Mizlbrak had no such qualms and was more than happy to provide her with the requested information.

That task complete, Niska set about finding something to satiate her growing appetite. She enjoyed a few "free" samples, liberated by her deft hands before purchasing two meals from a vendor serving a dish of fried rice and glazed duck, coated in an orange sweet and spicy sauce. She tossed in an extra silver to get two small skins of chilled blueberry fusion drinks. Niska was a bit confused when the vendor gave her two sets of tiny sticks along with her meal, but she did not say anything as she saw how others were using the sticks to scoop food from their plate.

Her mouth watering with anticipation, Niska was happy to find an eating nook just around the corner. Niska arrived in the eating area just as a worker was picking a table upright and arranging a few chairs that had been carelessly thrown aside. The young lad looked at the burvore and flashed her a warm smile. "Sorry about the delay, little lass, but there was a bit of a dust up in here a short while ago. But don't you worry, this market is one of the safest places in Sunder's Dawn, so please have a seat and enjoy your meal." With that, the man gave a practiced bow and quickly excused himself.

Niska waited a moment as the boy walked further into the market. She then went to one of the tables in the back corner and laid out her two meals, before reaching into her splinter sac to bring Z'har back to her side.

"I was starting to think that you had forgotten about me," quipped Z'har as sweat glistened off of his lean arms. "I was just getting into the groove of a nice workout when your giant hand comes groping in to scoop me out of my imprisonment."

"Oh, I'm so sorry," mocked Niska, as she waved her hand over the table of food in an exaggerated gesture. "I mean, I can eat all of this on my own if you wish to go back in the sac and finish your martial training."

"Well, I wouldn't go that far," laughed Z'har who was even then sitting down at the table and reaching for a plate of food. "It's just that it always looks so funny to see a giant hand materializing out of nowhere. Also, what are these?" Z'har enquired as he picked up two of the tiny sticks.

"I guess that's what passes for eating utensils around here," Niska answered as she tried to mimic the others, she had seen using them. After a few failed attempts, she gave up and pulled a fork out of her backpack. She then rolled her eyes in mock irritation, as she watched Z'har using the sticks with ease.

"Show off," Niska said, knowing that Z'har's knack for quickly learning new skills was a product of his zin nature.

"What can I say," Z'har began. "I'm just good at… basically everything," he finished with a chuckle.

Their merriment was cut short as a mother entered the eating nook with a child in tow. She took one look at Z'har and clutched her child close, as if the elf before her was a demon from the darkest forest of Demmis. The human female could be overheard saying, "Since when did they start letting those pointy ears in this place?" as she hastily made her exit from the eating area.

"Sorry," said Niska as she watched the cheer bleed from Z'har's face.

"It's not your fault," responded Z'har as he turned his attention back to his meal.

The two ate in silence for a while, before Niska filled the void with an update on her day and what she had learned. They agreed to finish eating and go straight to Faldrin's Anvil. Hopefully they wouldn't encounter any more bigotry in the town, but neither of them was very hopeful on that score.

No more than forty minutes later, Niska and Z'har rounded the corner on Hemlock Road and stared across at Faldrin's Anvil. Both could appreciate the dwarven craftsmanship evident in the stout building's construction. Z'har, whose cowl was pulled up to hide his elongated ears and elven features, thought the shop looked a bit out of place as it was sandwiched between two, much taller, structures built of wood. In fact, Faldrin's Anvil was the only building on that side of the street made of stone.

The pair quickly made their way down the street and ducked in through Faldrin's Anvil's solid oak door who's elegantly decorated painted glass window depicted a handsome dwarf working at the forge. The inside of Faldrin's Anvil was well-maintained and contained a variety of weapons and armor that were strategically displayed around the large open room. Niska quickly scanned the room, taking note of the thick metal cylinders installed over the main door and the establishment's two large windows. She recognized them from her time in Skyfall. It was a unique construct of drek and dwarf design, which housed a segmented metal grate that could be hastily lowered over the doors and windows during times of trouble. She had not expected them to be used outside of Skyfall, as she had never seen them anywhere else.

Besides, him and Niska, Faldrin's Anvil had three customers who were deep in conversation with a tan-skinned shield dwarf. From the sound of it, it seemed as if the three were trying to outbid one another over the purchase of a rather splendid looking longsword. If Z'har's Oromo (the languages primarily used by merchants) was correct, then it looked like the tall, three-eyed, drek was the woman to beat. The elf assumed the drek must have a separate buyer lined up as dreks were not known for their love of war and this one didn't look like she had ever held a sword, much less used one in battle. *Careful,* he thought, *don't jump to conclusions. For all you know she could be the very Mistress of Death herself,* he concluded, referencing an old fable he had once heard.

"Welcome to Faldrin's Anvil!" chirped a pale skinned dwarf with long brown hair pulled back into a thick bun, that had stepped around the counter and was approaching them with a warm smile on his face. "I must say we don't get too many wolvn burvores in these parts. Oh, it is common to get a few ottens from time to time, since there is a small colony of those water-breathers that make their home in a nearby section of the Indorra River. And what have we here?" he continued as he allowed his vision to pierce the shadows of Z'har's cowl. "An elf?" queried the dwarf whose smile grew even wider, and who's proffered arm was a welcome invite. "Trovkil Anvil at your service. How can we be of service to you today?"

Z'har clasped the dwarf's forearm, returning the

standard greeting, feeling the tension drain from his shoulders with the action. "My companion and I have traveled from Skyfall at the request of Mihoko Nurak. She indicated that we might learn some information to assist on our current course."

"Ah, then you must be Z'har, and your friend with the roving eyes, would be Niska," the dwarf retorted. "We hadn't expected you guys for at least another tenday or two. I'm glad to see you made the journey safely." Lowering his voice, and taking a step closer to the pair, Trovkil continued in perfect Elf Tongue, "We have learned more about the problem you face and should be able to point you in the right direction, but that is best discussed when there are not prying eyes around. We are expecting one more customer to come and pick up some armor that Faldrin has prepared for her, but should be closing in less than an hour. You could wait in here, or sit in our private waiting room, which is just around the corner in the covered alley."

"I think we'll check out the waiting area," said Z'har, appreciating the warmth of the dwarf's generosity, which contrasted the chilly reception he had come to expect from the citizens of the Archstone Range.

"Very well. Just give me one second," said Trovkil as he disappeared behind a set of doors near the counter. Within a few minutes he returned with a small sack, which he handed to Niska. "Take this. There are some sweet treats and two canteens of water inside. It should help ease some of the roughness of the road from your young bones," the dwarf finished as he laughed at his own joke.

"Much appreciated," responded Niska, who didn't get the joke, but was grateful for the dwarf's open nature.

The two turned right as they exited the store and

walked towards the corner of the building. They were just rounding the corner, no more than twenty-five paces from the main door, when a well-dressed man with curly blonde hair and a newly tailored long coat rudely rounded the corner. The man's eyes shot wide open and his face scrunched up into an ugly scowl, before he spat at Z'har's feet and shouted, "Stinking elf, go back and hide in the dank trees where you belong!"

Z'har's mood went from sunshine to storm cloud as he took a step towards the pompous fool, but a calming hand wrapped around his arm, and Niska softly stated, "Not now, we're too close to learning what is going on with the vlel child. We can't risk doing anything to get chased out of town at the moment."

Z'har glanced at his furry friend, then back at the laughing human, just as the man began to walk past a beautiful elon female and her smaller human companion. To Z'har's surprise, the elon stepped towards the human and shoved him, sending him flying off the covered walkway to sail several feet through the air before landing in the street. The man's expression was one of disgust as his fine clothing was stained with a mixture of dirt and urine from horses that were tied in front of Faldrin's Anvil. Following, Niska's insistent lead, Z'har ducked into the alley but did not miss the mocking laughter that ushered from several others on the streets.

"Serves him right," chuckled Niska, glad to see Z'har also smiling over the turn of events.

"That elon was quite something," Z'har stated. The tone in his voice making it clear to Niska that he admired more than the elon's gallantry and easy confidence.

"Don't get any ideas, old man," Niska said with a

smirk. "We have a mission here, and it is not to see if your legendary charms extend beyond the valley." This last part dripped with sarcasm, causing Z'har to roll his eyes as he followed his friend down the alley, which was covered by a wooden roof, cleverly designed to allow rainwater to funnel to the sides and lead into two large barrels on either side of the walkway.

About thirty feet into the alley, sat a stone structure with rectangular cutouts fitted with some type of metal mesh that appeared to be more screen than window. Z'har knew enough about construction to infer from the coloration of the mortar, that this building must be a recent addition to Faldrin's Anvil. As he and Niska passed through the doors, he could see that the small room was well-appointed. Two stout wooden chairs and a long couch, covered with plush furs, were pushed against two of the walls. In the center of the room was a small round table, with a candle and flint and steel resting upon it. The outline of a door, leading into Faldrin's Anvil proper could be seen a few feet from the couch. The door was covered with a thick gray curtain, which Z'har surmised was put there to keep construction dust from the pouring into the door.

"This place ain't half bad," Niska intoned as she spread out on the couch and started rifling through the sack of treats. After picking out a few for herself, she tossed the sack to Z'har, who had pulled one chair to face the other and was sitting with his legs stretched across both.

"Can't say that it is," Z'har responded over a mouth full of sweet delights. "Then again, I would expect nothing else from dwarves." Since elves and burvores both have star-sight and could see very well in low light conditions, neither of them opted to light the candle. Instead, they enjoyed the calming darkness that enveloped them like a comforting blanket.

"Psst," whispered Niska, as she gently nudged her friend's shoulder. She regretted having to wake Z'har as she knew how little sleep the elf had gotten over the last few months. However, recent activity in the alley took precedence over a proper rest.

A few minutes ago, seven hooded figures came stalking past the small room. None looked into the room, and so did not seem to be aware of Niska or Z'har. Always curious, Niska watched the group from the safety of the shelter. The men stopped about halfway between Niska's hiding place and the alley's exit. They seemed to be waiting for something, and judging by the way they readied their weapons were anticipating a fight.

"The tall oak bird's right to be plucked, but the fire bird's aiming for the poker," spoke one of the hooded figures in a deeply resinous voice. "Just wait till Migdla, pipes the tweeter, afore we give the jizz our splat."

Niska was versed in many languages, including Thieves' Cant, and so was able to discern that these men were planning to attack the elon and her red-haired friend. The plan was to kill the elon, and something even worse for the young girl. While Niska didn't know who these men were, and she was certain they must all be male, she knew she could never leave anyone to such a fate, and so figured that Z'har might be able to release some of his pent-up frustration after all.

"You were right to wake me," whispered Z'har after Niska explained what was going on. He unsheathed his sword, then silently followed the burvore out of the door. The day's sun was waning at this late hour and the covered alley was bathed in deep shadow. The two had no trouble sneaking close to their quarry, who were all staring out of the alley, seeking a signal to spring their attack.

Just then, a body fell out of the sky and crushed a man standing there. The toughs in the alley jumped in surprise over the demise of their fellows, and thus missed the actions of the burvore as she caused tendrils of stone to shoot out the Anvil's walls to clamp around the legs, arms and mouth of one of the men and pull him tight against the stone building. A second would be attacker was turning his head to investigate the strange gurgling sounds of his comrade when Z'har burst from the shadows and bashed him in the face with the butt of his sword. He then turned in a backward arc, while sweeping out his right leg to knock the man from the ground. He then leapt upon the prone man and delivered a heavy blow with his left hand. The stunned man went limp as his consciousness sent him hiding somewhere in the dark.

"By Lor's sometimes whiskers!" shouted one of the men as he spied what was going on. "Looks like them birds might have had friers in the henhouse," he continued as he lowered his shoulders and barreled into Z'har, knocking the elf back several paces.

"More geese for the pot," uttered the largest of the group, who then sucked in a deep breath and spewed out a stream of molten rocks, that cracked and blistered within the confines of the alley. Anticipating the actions of his fellow, the man confronting Z'har had already dropped to his belly. Seeing the coming blast, Z'har leaped up and stretched himself out horizontally to avoid most of the blast. The elf was bashed by some of the heated mass and grimaced as pain radiated down his back. Z'har completed his aerial dance, but was forced to duck and dodge as the other man stood up and swung at him with a heavy hammer.

The hooded figure with the breath weapon, tossed back his hood, allowing Niska to see his rorgn features. Niska had experience training with, and battling half dragons and so was not put off when this one rushed her position. She retreated a few paces down the alley, allowing the large rorgn to get closer to her, before reaching out with her zin power to cause a spike of wood to shoot down from the alley's roof. The spike impaled the rorgn's left thigh, ripping a howl of pain from his throat, even as two of his comrades rushed by to confront the retreating burvore.

A faint bluish mist erupted from Z'har's skin as two massive hounds appeared in the alley. As they were psychically linked with Z'har, Bodica and Zion were well aware of the situation and immediately set upon the two unsuspecting men advancing on Niska. Zion mauled the nearest man, carrying him to the ground under her immense weight, while Bodica slashed the second man's sword arm, sending his weapon into the darkness. Niska took advantage of the man's distraction and stepped in aiming a savage kick between the man's legs.

Seeing Niska's actions out of the corner of his eye, Z'har winced in sympathy for the man, even as the elf ducked under the wild swing of his opponent before sending the flat of his blade to bludgeon the man's skull. He then kicked out with his right leg, catching the man in the face and causing him to fall limply to the ground.

Upon seeing the swift way his comrades were dealt

with, the last man turned and headed for the alley's exit. A savage howl sounded from somewhere on the street, as Z'har looked at Bodica and said, "Go."

The hound gave an answering howl as he bounded after the fleeing man. The large chaga hound quickly overtook the man who had turned the corner and was running all out down an empty street. Bodica scooped the man up in his powerful jaws, but did not bite down with killing force, as he sensed that Z'har had no desire to see the man dead. However, the man was not aware of the hound's magnanimous nature and began stabbing at it with his dagger. One wild swing pierced Bodica's eye, causing him to yelp in pain and drop the man from his mouth.

A sudden irritation in his left eye, made Z'har aware of Bodica's injury. He looked at Zion, who released a low growl, indicating that she too felt the pain of her lover. The enraged chaga hound needed no prompting from the elf, as she sped to Bodica's aid. Seeking the most direct route, Zion phased through the walls of Rook's Clothier as well as the building across the way, barely breaking stride as she burst onto the scene and crushed the head of Bodica's attacker with one bite from her powerful jaws. She then strolled up to Bodica and licked at his injured eye, even as blue mist formed around them both, ushering them from Mythandria and back to their home plane.

"Well, it sounds like you've had a busy day and have likely made no small share of enemies in Sunder's Dawn," said Faldrin after hearing the tale of their two guests. "And you say, these men all had an X tattoo on their face? Are you sure they won't get out of their bonds?" he continued, casting a knowing glance at Trovkil

"Yes, and yes," answered Niska. "Their bonds will last for several more hours before dissolving," she added, knowing the nature of the creations she was able to manifest out of the surrounding elements. "We also took the liberty of stashing them behind a few large crates, so hopefully no one will happen upon them in the interim."

"Good thinking, that," Faldrin said, standing from the chairs in which they were all sitting. The dwarf started to walk towards a wall at the back of the shop. He continued speaking as the others fell into step behind him, "Well, that means our window is shorter than expected. I was able to cobble together some information from what Mihoko told me of your experience in Skyfall, but we'll need the aid of the spirits to get us any further."

As they approached the wall, Niska noted that Z'har hadn't rubbed at his eye in several minutes. This was a good sign that Bodica was healing well, now that the hounds were back on their home plane. She watched as Faldrin turned to Z'har and looked him in the eyes. "Before we go any further, I need to know if any powerful spirit has marked you as an enemy. If so, I will have to apply more wards to safeguard us all as we proceed."

"I have not had a ton of dealings with spirits, and don't believe that any care about me one way or the other," Z'har answered honestly.

"Very well," said Faldrin who placed his right hand on an indistinct section of the wall, causing an enchanted glyph to appear on its surface and a portion of the nearby wall to fade, revealing a circular room beyond. "After you," stated the dwarf as he proffered a courtly bow and stepped aside to allow them entrance. Both of the guests could feel the magic emanating from that room, but only hesitated for the merest of moments before stepping forth.

Chapter 5:
Ahoy the Camp

The night was dark as the trio sped away from Sunder's Dawn. Ivara experienced a pang of guilt as her hand brushed the side of her horse's neck and she felt its muscles quiver beneath her. She knew it was reckless to ride horses so fast in the dark and that it was terrible on the horses for her to have pushed them so hard. She risked a glance back, past Feri whose expression held a sordid mixture of fear and excitement, to gaze upon Grim. The set of the dwarf's jaws indicated he understood the danger they were in, but that he would follow her lead in this matter even though he had much more experience than she. Ivara silently thanked the dwarf for that, but knew it was time to call a halt all the same.

"Woah there," Ivara stated as she gently pulled on the reigns of her charging steed. The black and brown mare immediately responded to her prompt by slowing to a slow canter, breathing heavily all the while.

"Do you think we are safe?" asked Ferika as her horse pulled up beside Ivara's.

"We've been riding long and hard," answered Grimlocke, before sliding off his horse and walking beside it. The dwarf's wings were once again draped around him like the fabric of a supple cloak. He cast a glance back the way they came and viewed only hills and trees. "We are many leagues from Sunder's Dawn and can afford to slow down. Besides, the horses were just as likely to fall over from exhaustion, or break leg on this uneven ground if we had continued on at such a break-neck pace."

"We're better off looking for a place to camp for the night, and then move out as soon as the light touches the land," Ivara interjected. The elon cast her glance around, trying to locate an area that would suit their needs. The immediate landscape didn't seem to offer any chance for them to hide themselves as they rested, but maybe there was something further ahead.

"I'll take a look about," Grimlocke said while flexing his wings. "I haven't been in the region in some time, but I seem to recall a series of rocky outcroppings near a sizeable stream somewhere in these parts. I'll be back soon," the dwarf finished as he launched himself into the air and soon disappeared into the distance.

"You handled yourself pretty well," Ivara said as she and Ferika dismounted and continued to walk the horses into the gloom. "I'm glad to see them Keltans didn't make you too soft," she chided in a jovial manner.

"Thanks, I guess," responded Ferika. "We Keltans wouldn't have such a fearsome reputation if we weren't good fighters. But then again, I guess that's why I don't consider myself a good Keltan. I know it had to be done, but fighting is the last thing I ever want to be doing. That's why the Society of Alms seems like the perfect fit for me."

Keeping one eye on their surroundings, Ivara half

turned to glance at the young Keltan. "Hear me Feri, and hear me well. This world is harsh and often unforgiving. It is good that you have a kind heart, but don't let that leave you dead in a ditch somewhere. There are times when words and soft actions can get you out of a situation, but I have found it is often brute force that gets the swifter resolution. I know the healers of the Society teach all that peace and love stuff, but never forget peace must often be defended by force."

"Maybe you're right," retorted Ferika as she watched Grimlocke swoop back into view. "I guess that's why the Society of Alms makes each of us initiates spend time wondering the land. Maybe they too feel that we have to learn the harder lessons of the world so we may better understand the needs of those we will one day serve."

"Sounds about right," supposed Ivara, whose starsight offered her a better view of the smile on Grimlocke's face. "It looks like our feathered friend has found something that has him in good spirits."

The winged dwarf landed close to Ivara and Ferika and walked over to take the reins of his horse. "Well, it looks like someone made a lasting impression on a few gentlemen from Sunder's Dawn," Grimlocke quipped. He sent a sly wink Ferika's way before gesturing towards Ivara and continuing. "This one has them two helpful lads so enthralled that they just had to see her once more. Well, I can't speak for the short one, but that tall fella Mel, yeah he's smitten for sure."

"What are you talking about, bird brain?" asked Ivara, more curious than annoyed.

"You'll see," answered Grimlocke as he led the group into the night.

A short while later, the trio stood before a comfortable looking campsite with five tents spread out in a wide circle around a central fire, over which a deer was being slowly cooked. Mateo hunched over the fire tending to the meat, while Mel worked closely beside him mixing ingredients of onions, potatoes, carrots and an array of spices together in a large pot. The smell of the food brought smiles Ferika and Grimlocke's faces, but the smile that bloomed on Ivara's face sprung from a different source.

As the trio approached, Mel straightened and turned their way, but had eyes only for the beautiful elon. "Ah, my wait is over, for I once again can gaze upon the radiance of your visage." His melodious voice rumbled like the distant waves and threatened to carry Ivara away into unknown depths. Stepping forward, Mel dipped in a low bow, extending his hand of invitation to the group.

"What mi hermano is trying to say, is that he owes me five of those gems in his pouch, because it was my guess that placed us here at the time of your passing," Mateo spoke without turning from his task. "So there we were, sitting peacefully in our estate, when Mel starts bellyaching about how much he would like to see the lovely Ivara again and that he may have missed his one and only chance at true love."

"I think, I put it a fair bit better than that," Mel said, smiling as he tossed several large gems at his brother, who deftly caught all of them with one hand, while skewering the meat with a long fork.

"Regardless of how it went," continued Mateo, "I

was the one that deduced this would be your avenue of retreat from our fair town. And what luck, this deer was just hanging out, practically asking to be gutted and thus can we offer you a wondrous repast."

Taking Mel's offered hand, Ivara allowed herself to be escorted over to a felled tree that they used as a makeshift bench. The darkness of the night could not diminish the handsomeness of Mel's features, nor the smoldering delight of his eyes. Ivara's lips curled into a seductive smile, which revealed the barest hint of her sharp eyeteeth. "You went through all this trouble, just for me? Whatever will I do to repay you?" Ivara purred into Mel's ears.

"Well, I can think of at least one or two things," Mel whispered, letting his breath caress Ivara's neck, sending an involuntary shiver through her body.

"Get a tent, you two," laughed Mateo as he began to carve up the meat.

"I do believe that is the plan," said Ivara as she stood up and led a willing Mel to a tent further away from the rest.

"Okay, dinner anyone," said Mateo to Grimlocke and Ferika, who were seeing to the horses.

"I guess that's a meal for three. I don't expect we'll be seeing them for a while," chuckled Grimlocke as he sensed the application of magic, and surmised it was some type of privacy spell emanating from a particular tent. He knew Ivara's feran nature always had her libido up after a battle and figured Mel was just the answer to the elon's unspoken prayers.

"Yup, that food smells divine and I'm suddenly very hungry," retorted Ferika. Grimlocke was happy to see that Feri didn't seem bothered by the openness of Ivara and Mel. He understood that even though she was young, Feri was from Kelitan and likely had seen many open displays of sexuality through the years.

The trio shared an enjoyable meal and then sat around the fire sharing stories. Quite some time later, they were joined by Ivara and Mel, who tucked into the food as if there were no tomorrow. The two kept exchanging glances and smiles as they finished off a good portion of the remaining fare.

The night sky was clear and the fire kept the bulk of the chill away. Ferika sat close to Grimlocke, who wrapped her with one of his wings, sending her into past memories of her childhood. Only then did Ferika realize how much she had missed Grimlocke, Ivara and even Cavazos. The three adventurers often visited her home village as they sought out some ancient burial ground or another. They had grown close to her parents who would sometimes accompany them on their quest for plunder, and thus had got to know little Feri as she grew up. When the elders of the Society of Alms sent the initiates away so they could spend time in the wider world, Ferika could think of no better companions to explore with, than these.

Ferika was just about to doze off, when the pressure from Grimlocke's wings changed as he shifted to get a better look at Mel. The tall human went from jokes to all business as he extracted himself from Ivara's embrace and stood up, staring off into the night's sky. Neither Grim or Ivara seemed to be able to see what had drawn Mel's attention, but Mateo clearly was equally concerned as he took several steps away from the fire and also looked into the empty sky.

"Amigos," Mateo whispered, as a dagger manifested in each hand. "It appears we have attracted the attention of …something.

"I can't quite make it out," said Mel, "but it is headed this way and fast. I suggest you prepare yourselves."

"Your eyes must be much sharper than mine, because I can't see anything out there," responded Grimlocke as he nevertheless stood up and called forth the bow from his enchanted tattoo. He looked to Feri and Ivara, who were equally as confused, but also wisely produced weapons and took up a defensive stance outside of the sphere of light cast by the fire.

The minutes seemed to slowly tick away as the group watched the night's sky in silence. Grimlocke could feel the tingle of powerful spells being cast, and though they were too powerful for him to identify without further effort, he assumed they were protective spells cast by one of the two brothers.

"Wait, is that a …a flying dog?" asked Mel as he turned to his brother with a puzzled look on his face.

"No sey," answered Mateo as he was genuinely stumped by the sight that was slowly coming into view. "It looks like a winged dog carrying a brownie and a gnome. That is something you clearly don't see every day."

"Hold them daggers of yours," barked Grimlocke as the strange apparition finally came into his view. The dwarf's tone was light hearted as he allowed the magic of his bow to expire. "Them there ain't no threat. The gnome is Cavazos, a member of our small fellowship and longtime friend. The mount and brownie are less well known to me, but are no enemies, to be sure."

"How'd that old earth hugger find us out here?" asked Ivara as she walked closer and laid a calming hand on Mel's muscular back. "Wasn't he supposed to meet us in Kriasta a month from now?"

"That was the plan," replied Grimlocke as he walked over and checked the pot to ensure there was still more food to be had. "But since he is traveling with Itsumi and Bella, I am sure there is a tale to be heard. I'm just glad there's still some food left because that one is always ready for a meal."

The dwarf watched as the bulldog landed over two hundred feet from the camp, and was not surprised to hear Cavazos call out, "Ahoy the camp, weary travelers have come a callin with no animosity in our hearts or weapons in our hands. May we approach yonder fire and share the warmth of story and shelter?"

"Aye," answered Ivara as she strolled toward her dear friend, voicing her response to the standard greeting between strangers on the road. "Although I must admit it was quite a shock to see Bella soaring out of the darkness as we are nowhere near Kriasta, which is where we were supposed to be meeting up with you," she finished as she bent low to give Cavazos a hug. The old gnome was practically swamped beneath Ivara's large frame, but did manage to return a squeeze of his own.

"The battle for Chaluk'Sen is going much better than anticipated, and just when I was thinking it would be nice to take a few tendays to rest my weary bones, this little trouble maker, and her curious hound came to whisk me on yet another mission for Mother Midnight," Cavazos intoned as Bella returned to normal size and rushed to bathe Ivara in slobbery kisses. The bulldog's tail was a constant blur as the elon scooped her up and gently rubbed her belly.

"You know you shouldn't do that," chided Itsumata in a jovial tone. "It's hard for me to convince people that Bella is a vicious beastie when she's all love and hugs with you."

"Bah, Itsumi, I'll hear no such talk," smirked Grimlocke as he too came over to greet his friends. The dwarf offered his hand for the diminutive brownie to clamber up on before raising her to rest on his shoulders. "You may have the world convinced about the deadliness of your canine companion, but we know the truth. A little belly rub and some good grub is all it takes to win that one over."

"Maybe so," responded Itsumata, as she turned towards the advancing brothers. "That may be true, but we have to maintain appearances, especially in the presence of strangers."

"Apologies," said Mateo who stopped several paces away and sketched an elegant bow. "Your secret remains ever safe with mi hermano and I, for rarely have we ever seen such a fearsome specter as your four-legged friend."

Ivara was a little surprised to hear Mateo speaking Cholu as if he were born of the People. It was not common to hear that tongue spoken by many outside of Chaluk'Sen. She quickly put that thought aside after considering how capable the brothers appeared to be in other aspects. She introduced the brothers, but knew Cavazos was only half listening as he was again buried beneath another affectionate hug, this time by Feri whose smile split her face in beauteous delight.

After the pair separated, Cavazos introduced Itsumata and Bella to Ferika and the brothers. They then all sat around the fire and exchanged stories as the newcomers finished up the last of the prepared food.

Not too long after that, Mateo stood and stretched before saying to the group, "Well amigos it has been fun getting to know you, but I'm afraid mi hermano and I must be off. Given your evening's exploits, I fear that Sunder's Dawn is in for a time of turmoil. Even now, I can see that your exit did not go unnoticed, since there are about fifteen, ...no, eighteen Xrs streaming past the gates heading this way."

"But how do you kn...," began Ferika, voicing the thoughts of her companions.

"No es nada," interjected Mateo, waving the still-born question away with the ease of a practiced orator, "Some things are easy to see if only you know how to look. I'm thinking that maybe we'll use this opportunity to get off the fence and make some much-needed changes in Sunders Dawn."

"My brother does love his secrets," Mel whispered into Ivara's ear, his breath causing goosebumps to appear along the elon's neck. The tall human gently kissed Ivara on the cheek before standing and addressing his brother. "I'm not so sure about all that last part. It may be best to let things percolate a bit to see what the new landscape might look like before determining how best to shape it to our own designs." Turning once more to Ivara, he continued, "My dear lady, with your permission we would be more than willing to handle the issue of your ardent pursuers so that you can spend the rest of the night in peace."

"Oh, so you got it like that?" asked Ivara, only slightly joking. She was intrigued by the easy grace of the brothers and their apparent confidence in their own abilities. While she had not seen them in battle, she knew that Mel was master of at least one art. But who were they really, to so casually discuss altering the power structure of an entire town? "Suit yourself," she smirked. "After all, I think I've had enough exercise tonight."

"Can there every really be enough?" questioned Mel, as his brother gave an exaggerated sigh and put his head in his hand in mock annoyance. Unperturbed, pulled a necklace out of his belt pouch and handed it to Ivara. "My heart breaks because I must leave you so soon. Though I suppose your road will take you far from here, I am confident we will see each other again. Perhaps you would wear this as a token of my affection and as a remembrance of me. It may provide you luck when the need is most dire."

"That is sweet," responded Ivara as she placed the lovely necklace around her neck, and examined its intricately designed dragon's head amulet that nestled between her breasts. She imagined she could feel the flow of a protective enchantment ebbing from the amulet, but the sensation was gone nearly as swiftly as it arrived.

"I would say, get a room. But, como no, I know we don't have time for that," chortled Mateo as he started out into the darkness.

"Too true, brother of mine," said Mel as he gave Ivara a last kiss and said his goodbyes to the rest of the group. "Oh, you can have the use of the tents through the night. Just leave them there in the morning and they will be taken care of." With that, Mel joined his brother as the two made their way back to Sunder's Dawn.

Later that same night, Cavazos dreamt he was soaring through the sky on the back of a massive vyrrum, arguably the largest variety of dragon native to Mythandria. The obsidian dragon had a long serpentine body and with no legs, two muscular arms, and powerful wings that carried them high on the cool currents of wind. The pair streaked towards a cloud ladened horizon, that seemed to always remain one wing's thrust out of touch. Suddenly, a great stream of lightning split the heavens, followed immediately by a thunderous boom that reverberated through Cavazos' brain like the gong of a tower bell.

The serpentine black dragon banked left, to avoid a finger of white electricity, but was not quick enough. Roaring in pain, the vyrrum faltered in its flight as one of its wings was punctured by the force of the impact. The world spun a chaotic vortex of motion as Cavazos, having been flung free of the falling dragon, sped towards the ground. Spells to extract him from the peril flashed through the gnome's mind, but none would respond to his call. A second rumble of thunder issued behind him, and as the gnome smashed into the canopy of the trees below a shout of pure terror escaped his gaping mouth. In desperation, Cavazos threw up his hands in an attempt to shelter his face from the impending impact with the ground... that never came.

Instead, the old gnome found himself standing on shaky legs in a gloomy forest of twisted trees and strange beasts. Thunder boomed again, but this time it did not emanate from the sky. No, the sound of thunder came from the ground, the trees, and the very air around him. The thunder's rhythmic bombardment grew in intensity with every passing moment, threatening to overcome Cavazos' senses. But the noise ceased as suddenly as it had appeared, and the gnome was left standing in an open field as sunflowers swayed in the night's breeze.

Before him loomed a door that stretched into the heavens and beyond. But that was not what drew the gnome's attention and had him taken cautious steps backward. For standing at the door was a creature of pure nightmare, whose inky-black outline seemed to shift and flow like the waters of some great waterfall. To his dismay, the gargantuan creature turned its attention on the diminutive Cavazos with something of recognition in its eyes. A cruel smile erupted along its gnarled lips like some volcanic flow from the darkest pits of Demmis. "What have we here? Do we detect the taint of Avri'Nvar in this piteous groundling?" hissed the being as it sent a hailstorm of dark tendrils snaking towards the gnome, whose petrified limbs would not respond to his desperate attempts to flee.

Death tickled Cavazos' soul as the tendrils touched his skin and began to pull him towards the dread horror. From within the gloom of the encompassing tentacles, Cavazos could feel, more than see, a small breach open within the door's structure. From the aperture erupted a thick beam of violet light that punctured the cocoon of tentacles, whisking Cavazos towards the opening. As Cavazos was being drawn into the opening, he could hear the creature let out a mighty snarl of rage and pound its myriad of fists against the door, sending another wave of thunder that was thankfully cut short, by the closing of the breach.

"Are you okay?" came the timid voice of the small vlel child, that had become so familiar to Cavazos.

"Yes," answered the gnome, although the shakiness of his voice wouldn't even convince him of the truth of that statement. "What was that?"

"I don't know," responded the girl who looked more exhausted than usual. "I think it has been getting closer each time I reach out to someone. The elf told me how to make the door to keep it out, but that was before he killed me again."

"What are you talking about?" inquired Cavazos as he took a step towards the child.

"I'm not really sure," the girl stated truthfully. "He was the first person that I was able to reach out to several months ago. He was here to save me, but always kills me in the end. I don't think it's his fault, you know. I don't think he wants to, but it still happens."

The sound of hammering at the door drew both of their attention from the odd conversation. "I don't have much time," the child squealed as anxiety creeped over her features, and the scene shifted once again.

This time, Cavazos found himself once again standing in a large audience hall looking out at the attendees. The appointment of the chamber reminded Cavazos of a stately castle and he swiveled his head to take in as much of the scene as he could. A hand swam into view from somewhere over his left shoulder and try as he might, the gnome could not turn his head to look in that direction. The pale hand snatched at the chain around the child's neck, eliciting a small whimper of pain. Cavazos could hear a voice issuing commands to the child, but could not ascertain their meaning. Obedient, the child lowered her eyes and pointed out into the crowd.

A great commotion ensued as the lios shakaran she pointed to leaped from his chair and made a dash for the door. Several other attendees tried to stop him, but the burly lion-like humanoid bowled them over with nary a thought. Then two men, dressed in lush furs emblazoned with an inverted triangle emblem, stepped into his path. One swept a staff in an underhand arc, that took the shakaran's feet from under him. The other threw enchanted manacles that landed on the prone shakaran and crawled along his body to clamp down on his wrist and ankles.

"Nicely done, my pet," slithered a sinister voice from out of the void behind him. Cavazos could only watch in despair as the hand yanked the child to her knees and stroked her hair as a master would his favorite hound.

The child sobbed into her tiny hands, as her weary voice blossomed in Cavazos' head. "Please hurry, I can't take much more of this and I'm so tired."

"I will do all that I…" Cavazos begin, but then a loud boom echoed across the chamber as great door shook and Cavazos found himself startled awake within one of borrowed tents.

"Wow, that is quite the tale!" exclaimed Ferika after hearing Cavazos retelling of his final battle in Chaluk'Sen and then the subsequent dream encounters with the child over the past three nights.

The group sat around the fire in the early hours of the day, having been woken by Itsumata, at the behest of Cavazos. The gnome looked older than he had the night before. There were clear bags under his eyes and a notable weariness in his movements. The group had sat in silence as Cavazos relayed the past events, sitting cross-legged with Bella in his lap.

"Yeah, that is why I came to find you guys. I know we had other plans, but this is something that I must do and so I am asking for your help as I seek out this child," Cavazos stated as he glanced at the others.

"You know my blade is with you, my friend," said Grimlocke.

"Well, it beats going to a birthday celebration of some stuffy aristocrat anyway," responded Ivara, before turning to Ferika and saying, "No offense intended."

"And none received," laughed Ferika. "I know my

uncle can be a bit boorish sometimes, especially when he is surrounded by all those oh-so-important dignitaries that he constantly goes on about, but he means well. Still, I'd rather spend my time trying to help someone as opposed to feigning interest in matters of state. Besides, we can always go to his celebration next year."

"Then it is settled," stated Itsumata, who stood up and motioned for Bella to come to her. "I'll take word to Falzadrin of your change of plans. It will be good to look in on the old rogue anyway." The brownie started gathering her things as she addressed Cavazos, "So where do you intend to start your quest to find this girl and to learn more about the dark menace that is seeking her?"

"I'm honestly not sure, but I hope finding one will lead me to the other. The only thing I know is she is in some sort of castle, and then there is this," Cavazos responded as he pulled out a scrap of parchment upon which he had sketched the inverted triangle emblem. "This is what I saw on the two warriors that trapped the shakaran. Are any of you familiar with it?" he added as he passed the parchment around.

"I could be mistaken, but it looks like the crest of the Mefmacon Clan," Ivara said as none of the others had any suggestions. "They are a family of hunters that occasionally trade with the Keltans. I've only seen them a few times, but get the impression they are a rough bunch of no-good cutthroats. If I recall correctly, they operate from some place called Tatoras, which is supposed to be in the Outlands."

"Well, this just keeps getting better and better," quipped Ivara as she stood up and headed for the horses. "We're off to find some unknown clan, in an unknown city, in the least explored and possibly most inhospitable region of the Archstone Range. What could possibly go wrong?"

"Cheer up little sister, I'm sure there will be plenty of fighting in our future," said Grimlocke as he doused the flames and helped the others strike the camp.

"That better be a promise," responded Ivara in a jovial tone as chortles could be heard from the others who were well aware of her love of combat.

Chapter 6:
A Meeting of Minds

The first thing Z'har noticed as he stepped into the hidden chamber within Faldrin's Anvil, was that the space within seemed much larger than should be possible, given the relative dimensions of the whole building. The room was easily three hundred paces across and was shaped like an oval, with two circular alcoves set opposite each other. One of the alcoves contained two desks and a wide table covered with beakers, half-filled jars, and other oddities he could not recognize. The other was empty, except for the pentagram decorated on its floor. From this angle, Z'har could not make out much detail but could surmise that particular section of the room was used for summoning denizens of other planes.

As they proceeded further into the large room, Z'har could see the walls were covered in twelve-foot-tall bookshelves of darkly stained oak. Above the bookshelves, evenly spaced glyphs were carved into the wall. While Z'har was versed in several different languages, his ability to read them all was not without flaws. However, he knew enough about linguistics to recognize that Mage Tongue, Dwarf Tongue, and Techan were amongst some of the runes represented on the wall. There were still others, but Z'har could not even guess at their origins.

Several workbenches were spread about the massive space, but remained clear of the elaborate hexagonal design carved into the floor at the center of the room. As the group approached the hexagon, Z'har could feel the taint of old magic wafting from the myriad of runes enshrined in the marble floor. Faldrin held up his hand, causing Z'har and Niska to stop several paces removed from the hexagon. Together, they watched as Trovkil walked around the design and headed for a set of closed double doors at the opposite end of the room from where they had entered.

"I wish we had more time to offer you a proper visit," intoned Faldrin, breaking the silence that had descended upon the place. "However, given the situation with the Xrs it is probably best we see what we can learn of your quest and make plans to get you safely away from Sunder's Dawn before the gang can put out a bounty for your heads."

"Yes, I have grown quite attached to this one and would even hate to see his ugly mug removed from his body," joked Niska as she motioned towards Z'har, who simply rolled his eyes in response.

Before any of them could respond, Trovkil entered the room again followed by a cow on a thick lead. Z'har could see the dwarf had pulled back his brown hair into a ponytail that descended hallway down his back. As he walked, Trovkil began whispering words in an unfamiliar tone. Whatever he said seemed to agitate the cow, as its steps faltered and it began to attempt to back away. Yet, the strength of Trovkil would not be denied and the dwarf managed to maneuver the cow to the very center of the hexagon. Once there, Trovkil recited his chant once more and then swiftly stepped out of the hexagon as its runes flared to life and shot glowing beams towards the ceiling. As Z'har's eyes traveled up the rays of light, he saw that they merged with the runes of an identical hexagon carved into the room's oak-wood ceiling. The cow, whose struggle had escalated to a near panic now stood motionless, as if transfixed by unseen forces.

"Faldrin and I have been giving your situation considerable thought over the last few tendays," Trovkil stated when he was once again standing in from of Z'har and Niska. "After consulting several arcane sources, we believe that it may be possible to link minds with you so that we all may experience one of your vision dreams together. This would only be a temporary thing, allowing us to see what you see for just an hour or two, but hopefully that should be enough for us to gain further insight into what it is you face."

"Mihoko Nurak sent us your way, so whatever aid you can provide would be appreciated," answered Z'har, whose eyes alternated between the transfixed cow and the sturdy dwarf. "What exactly are you planning on doing? And what do you need of me?"

"From you, all we need is sleep. Faldrin will see to that." Trovkil responded, as Faldrin walked away from the group and began rummaging through a chest set against one of the walls. After a brief moment he pulled out a plush set of furs that he arranged into a sleeping pallet within the summoning alcove. "As for the rest of the process, our four-legged friend here will provide the necessary payment for a spirit guide who will link our consciousnesses and shepherd us through the ritual. This will enable us to see through your eyes, and to communicate with you, during your dream vision."

"Alright, let's get this over with," said Z'har who had

not had much dealings with spirits in the past, and was not exactly looking forward to the experience. He walked over to Faldrin, who handed him a small vile marked as Sleeping Potion, in dwarven letters.

"Cheer up, buttercup," Niska advised. "After all, you have the easy part. All you have to do is sleep. The rest of us have to wade through that thick skull of yours and try to come out sane on the other side."

"Ha, ha," Z'har replied dully as he took the potion and laid down on the furs, falling asleep within the next few breaths.

"You two should position yourselves in chairs, here and here," said Trovkil indicating spots outside of the alcove. "While we will not need to be sleep, the process might prove disorienting and I wouldn't want you to take injury from a fall or anything. I will remain standing as I have to be free to respond to any desires of our spirit guide."

As he spoke, Faldrin arranged the chairs in the desired spots and he and Niska took their seats. Trovkil then centered his mind and allowed his consciousness to enter the Spirit Realm. There, he was met by Sunziprix, a large bird-like spirit that was sent to aid him by Omihondrin, the dwarf's Animal Spirit Patron.

"Do you have my payment prepared?" squawked the spirit, getting down to business right away.

"Yes," answered Trovkil. "I have a nice plump cow just waiting to be bled. If there are no other questions, I will begin the ceremony."

"About that, for imparting the knowledge of this ritual, Omihondrin would like you to send the value of six thousand two hundred silver pieces to his agent Kriasta. It appears that one has encountered some trouble and needs a bit of coin to ease her path ahead."

"So, what else is new?" Trovkil chuckled. "Hetrolil is always getting into some kind of trouble. With all the silver I have sent her way, you'd think she could have bought half the land in the Archstone Range by this point. But fear not, I will do as requested."

With that, Trovkil allowed his consciousness to return to Mythandria. He then stepped into the inscribed hexagon and gently opened a small wound in the neck of the cow. Thick red blood began to flow from the wound and dropped towards the ground. However, the blood disappeared before reaching the floor as if devoured by an unseen force. After a brief moment, Sunziprix's form began to take shape as the bird-like spirit greedily consumed the life essence of the cow. Once Sunziprix had fully crossed over into the physical world, he released the magic needed to perform the planar crossing and placed his feathered hand over the cow, allowing the healing of a spell to close the wound. He then stepped before Trovkil, extended a taloned finger, and began carving an arcane symbol into the dwarf's head.

Though the dwarf knew what to expect from the ritual, he still did not enjoy the process and had to concentrate to keep himself still. It wasn't that the process was painful, for indeed he felt no pain at all from the spirit's work. What left Trovkil uneasy was that symbol linked his mind with those of Sunziprix and the other three within the room. The dwarf was bombarded by emotions, thoughts and memories that were not his own. From the burgeoning connection, the dwarf could feel the growing unease of the others, and was relieved when Sunziprix finished his carving and mentally imparted a feeling of peace that rolled through their connected minds like the gentle waves of an ocean.

Z'har found himself strolling through a dense jungle on a calm spring night. The gentle breeze of the wind tickled the hairs on the back of his neck as they played a sad melody through the surrounding leaves. The elf walked aimlessly through the woods, enjoying the peace of his surroundings. A peace that was violently interrupted as a myriad of confusion washed over him with the force of an angry sea. A host of memories and emotions swept through the elf's mind, threatening to bury him beneath their weight. But just as the pressure grew to a climax, he felt a soothing presence speak calm into his being.

Z'har gradually became aware of the presence of Niska and the others, even though he could not physically see them within his dream state. He was likewise aware their minds were linked and that the others would not be able to view and interact with him during his dream walk.

"Carry on, elf," came a voice that blossomed within Z'har's head. "Proceed as if we were not here."

And just that quickly, Z'har forgot about the others. The elf resumed his trip through the jungle and soon happened upon a small stream, which he crossed. On the other side, Z'har found himself strolling down a stone hallway with a series of barred doors on either side. As he watched, a vaguely humanoid shape opened the door to one of the cells and waited for Leloni to step out.

The vlel child looked even more frail than the last time Z'har saw her. Her slender shoulders slumped as she stood silently and let her handler attach the chain to the collar at her neck. Her sad eyes did spark with a moment of hope as she noticed Z'har standing there. But a second emotion flitted across her face and for the barest of moments Z'har witnessed pure terror bloom within the child.

"It's you again," she whispered. "Are you here to save me or to kill me?" she finished as the handler yanked her chain, forcing her to follow him towards the distant stairs. Z'har had been in enough of the dream walks to know he was witnessing what the vlel child was doing at this very moment, but that their communications were something only he and she could discern.

"I only wish to help you," Z'har said as a vision of him comforting the crying child in his arms danced into his head, only to be replaced by one of him chasing her through a field of tall grass and plunging his sword into her bare back. Z'har felt the shock and confusion that radiated across the mind link, but let it pass as the scene shifted. Z'har found himself standing beside the vlel, on a raised dais as they looked out into a crowd of supplicants.

"I… I thought you were here to help, but I… I don't know anymore," said the child, as her leash was violently yanked, causing her to turn her head and respond to the commands of her master.

"See who is holding her," Niska spoke into Z'har's mind.

The elf tried to turn his head to view the entirety of the scene, but only managed to glimpse the seated form of a tall figure upon an elaborate throne. He watched as a clawed hand reached out to grab hold of Leloni's hair and force her to peer into the audience. Z'har could make out no detail about her captor, save that her master's gray flesh seemed to be covered in tiny scales.

"The child is too afraid of her master to even allow

his visage within her dream walk," spoke Sunziprix. "I will have to intervene and go deeper into her mind than I had initially intended. The blood price will be higher than previously agreed."

"Make it so," came Trovkil's voice, along with a corresponding feeling of annoyance.

"I may be able to help you further," Z'har said to Leloni, as Sunziprix spoke through him. "But it may be unpleasant for you."

"What… what are you going to do?" asked the child, her rising fear evident in the timber of her voice.

"We will take a little journey through your past in the hope of identifying a clue that will help me find you. Don't worry, I will not allow you to come to any harm," finished the parroting Z'har.

Without waiting for a response, Z'har's body stepped closer to Leloni and he watched as his hands reached out to rest on either side of the girl's head. A small spark of pain burst to life within their shared consciousness, but swiftly faded as time and space shifted, depositing them within a dimly-lit field of tall grasses surrounded by soaring trees.

Bursting from behind their field of view, Z'har was stunned to see Borack rush forth carrying a bundle within his arms. His father's blue armor was dented in several places and was covered in crimson blood from various wounds. His breathing was shallow as he frantically swiped his sword at an unseen foe. A growl and anger and anguish could be heard from the surrounding trees, and Z'har and Leloni watched as a lean human female stepped into the clearing.

"Mother?" Z'har spoke, as his heart was flooded with a rush of emotions stemming from him and the mind-linked Niska.

The young elf watched in stunned silence as Winchunset hurled her enchanted mace at a wounded Borack, who just barely managed to turn his body so that he shielded his cargo from the blow. However, the force of the impact sent the bundle flying into the air as his body was blasted several feet to smash with a bone-crushing impact into a nearby tree.

The eyes of all the mind-linked watched as Winchunset sped across the distance at a speed that should not have been possible for a human. Catching the bundle in one clawed hand, the warrior turned and was surprised as three blazing arrows slammed into her body.

"You fools," shouted an enraged Winchunset with blood glistening from her pointy fangs, "Serafeen will not soon forget this betrayal."

Winchunset took a step towards her attackers, but was stopped as the enchantment of the arrows took effect and began burning her from the inside out. An ear-piercing screech of agony left her lips as a swarm of large rats engulfed her body, biting and scratching even as they dislodged the bundle from her arm and carried it into the growing gloom.

The scene shifted once more as a score of warriors on cadaverous steeds approached a tall moon-draped castle. The lead rider peered down at the bundle he carried and hissed at the crying child therein. "Such a tasty little morsel you would make," he whispered into the ear of the hungry babe.

"Master not be pleased, if harm this one," retorted a feral-featured vlel in tattered clothing that groveled before the mounted warrior.

"How dare you speak to me, you mangy cur!" the

warrior responded angrily as he kicked the mongruul vampire in the face, bursting its nose and sending it scurrying backwards. "Lord Tarakzin will have his pet, and I shall receive my reward."

The next few scenes pass in a blur, as the group observed the child being presented before a menacing figure who placed a collar on the babe's neck. Then, they watched as an elderly human female entered a dank cell and showed painted portraits to a child of perhaps five years. The child was told to plant particular thoughts within the minds of those in the portraits and was repeatedly beaten when she was unable to do so. Over time, the beatings become less frequent as the child aged and progressed in her mastery of her talents. She was taken to a cleaner cell and fed slightly better food, as an expression of her master's pleasure. However, the whip was never far from her back if she caused her master the slightest annoyance.

A loud screech, like the blinding cacophony of a thousand thunders, rumbled across their dreamscape, interrupting the scene and causing all of the viewers to turn outward. Beyond the castle walls, beyond the tall trees and many streams, they caught a glimpse of something monstrous on the horizon. A writhing mass of shadow and ash hung ponderously across the horizon, sinewy tendrils squirmed their way across the bloated expanse of putrid flesh that separated to reveal a creature with teeth and eyes too multitudinous to count, but all of which spoke of a hunger that could only be sated by more… of everything.

Pure terror flooded through Z'har as Sunziprix once again imposed his will over the elf's own. "By the gods of the Midnight House, can that be the Sunderer? If it is him, and he has designs on the child, then I fear she is all but dead," the spirit uttered before calming pausing to compose his thoughts. After a brief time, he addressed the other mind-linked ones. "We must depart from here as this place is no longer safe. If the Sunderer lives, then death will follow as his will is insatiable. …Yet, perhaps there is something I can do to help forestall his actions," he finished.

"Child," Z'har heard himself speak Sunziprix's words. "I can help you erect a barrier to keep this fiend at bay, but it will require that I perform a ritual to bind out Core against the approaching storm. Do you wish this to be so?"

"What, I…" began a clearly terrified Leloni, before firming her stance and saying. "Yes, please help. The darkness seems to get closer each time I see it."

"Very well," Z'har puppeted, as Sunziprix walked Leloni through the magical rites necessary to siphon some of Z'har's Core (the spark of divinity present within all beings of EverLore). During the process, Sunziprix intertwined the borrowed Core and the unusual power emanating from the child, with the currents of the Shadow Sea. The outcome was the creation of a magical barrier that took the shape of a mighty fortress door suspended in the air between the frightened child and the approaching cloud of chaos.

Just as the barrier blazed to life, the mind-link severed and Z'har and his companions were violently thrust out of the Dream Plane. Confused and disoriented, all of those in attendance, save Z'har, woke to find a clearly exacerbated Sunziprix hungrily devouring the life blood of the bleating cow.

Niska shook her head, trying to clear the cobwebs from her mind as she watched Faldrin walking towards the inscribed hexagon, supporting the weight of an obviously exhausted Trovkil.

"What was that?" asked Trovkil, his voice gradually strengthening as his senses fully returned to him. "Who, or what, is the Sunderer? And what role does he play in this mysterious affair?"

Tearing his beak from the gaping wound in the cow's neck, Sunziprix words slurred as if the avian spirit were drunk on the strongest ale. "Zyroon Kha is a mighty Shadow Born that sought to forge his own kingdom within the Shadow Sea. He was thwarted in his efforts by a host of powers that uncovered his plot before it reached its zenith. Infuriated by his defeat, and subsequent banishment from the Shadow Sea, the Sunderer vented his rage across the realm and is responsible for countless deaths. But this was more than five hundred years ago, and none have heard from him since. However, unless my eyes deceive me, I do believe that is what we have witnessed tonight. It would appear matters related to this child are more dire than I had conceived."

"Zyroon Kha," said Trovkil as he searched his brain for any memory of hearing such a name. "I have not heard of this Sunderer before, but will research the matter. What do you think his presence means? If he is as powerful as you indicate, then what could he possibly want with a little girl?"

"What he wants with the child, I cannot say. But it can't be good. He must be denied his prize at any cost. I will go to the Shadow Sea and consult with my contact there, as this is a threat well beyond my kin." With that, the spirit returned to his feast, ignoring any further questions until the cow was well and truly drained of blood, the empty meat-sack fell ponderously to the ground.

Unsure of what to do in the intervening moments, as Faldrin and Trovkil repeatedly bombarded the spirit with question after question that all went unanswered, Niska hurried to Z'har's side and gave a sigh of relief when she noticed the regular breathing of one deep in sleep. Her first thought was to shake her friend awake, but she hesitated as she was unsure why he was still asleep when the others had been forced awake.

"He will be fine otter-kin," stated Sunziprix, noting her concern, as he swiped a feathered hand across his scarlet-coated beak. "He will sleep the remainder of the night as his body needs time to heal from the draining of his Core. He will find it harder to tap into the flow of the Shadow Sea for at least a tenday and so I wouldn't rely on him to cast any spells in that time. But he is young, and will recover fully from the ritual. It is dirty business, that," the spirit said referring to the Core siphoning, "but I did what had to be done in the face of such an unexpected threat."

Over the next hour, the group discussed the dream vision they had witnessed. As Niska was unfamiliar with the Archstone Range, the fragments of glimpsed landscapes were meaningless to her. But the same could not be said of Faldrin, who found the visage of the moon-draped castle eerily similar to tales he had heard of a keep within the Outlands (a large swath of the Archstone Range that was mainly unexplored and home to many dangerous monsters). It was said the keep was home to an immortal fiend who ruled the land with infinite cruelty. While Faldrin could not be certain, he believed the keep's master was called Mayhubo Tarakzin.

Since that was the best guess they could come up with, a plan was devised on how to get Z'har and Niska safely away from Sunder's Dawn as they continued their journey to find the child from the dream. Faldrin would make arrangements to have the two join as guards on a wagon train that Sherkzin, their adopted daughter, was overseeing. The wagon train was set to leave in the morning and would wind its way through some of the smaller towns and villages in the area, before turning southeast towards Vizithia. The perspective route would take the pair to Beltzan, which is the last recognized city of the Archstone Range, that sits on the border of the unforgiving Outlands.

After bringing thick furs for Niska to make a pallet beside her friend, Faldrin left to notify Sherkzin she would have two additional blades for the protection of her caravan. He imagined she would be thrilled to get a chance to speak with the two, if for no other reason than to pick their brains about Mihoko Nurak, their relative from the Valley of Shale.

Trovkil removed the body of the cow and began mopping up the blood as he and Sunziprix continued conversing about other matters. Before the spirit departed from Mythandria, he came over and placed a vile in Niska's hands. He explained it was a sleeping drought of sorts, that would enable Z'har to get some much-needed rest, but would prevent him from entering the Dream Plane. This would give the elf and the vlel child time to contemplate all that has transpired and would hopefully give Z'har time to better prepare his mind for his next encounter with the mysterious child. The vile held enough concoction for six nights. Niska thanked the spirit for his aid, and soon drifted off to a dreamless sleep of her own.

Chapter 7:
The Deluge

The morning sun was high overhead as the three horses forded yet another shallow creek. The sound of the water flowing around their shod hooves, brought Ferika out of her daydream. The young human loved nature and often lost herself within the calm serenity birthed by a gentle breeze, the smell of sweet grass, and the warm rays of the sun. While she did enjoy her simple life back in the Grove of the Ancients, home to the Society of Alms, Ferika was happy for the chance to experience other parts of the world.

"You've been quiet for some time," stated the diminutive Cavazos, who sat in front of her on the saddle. "Where has your mind wandered to?"

"Nowhere, and everywhere," replied the teen as she looked around and wondered how much of the terrain had passed by without her mind truly registering it. "It's been a while since I have spent so much time on the open road. The trip to Sunder's Dawn was fairly uneventful and went by pretty much in a blur, but traveling with you three over the past few days has caused me to realize how much I truly miss being one with the world."

Looking around, Cavazos could only nod his head in agreement at the beauty of the land, but it was Grimlocke who responded, from his horse to their right. "The gods knew what they were doing when they fashioned the world. I sometimes wonder what the world would look like where it absent us sentient beings who often seek to dominate the land and bend it to our whims. That's one of the reasons I joined up with Old Man Cavazos, as it gave me an excuse to trapes around in ancient ruins that nature has reclaimed over the centuries."

"Huh," interjected Ivara as her horse once again stepped on dry land, "I'd be honoring Imsety if I said my motives for hanging with you two old farts was anything as altruistic as all that. No, for me, I'm in it for the wealth, freedom, and excitement that it offers."

"Far be it from you to pay homage to the Goddess of Lies," quipped Cavazos as their horse caught up to Ivara's. "I've heard you whisper more than a few prayers to Vanidor over the years, and bless his jeweled heart, but the God of Adventure never seems to let you down."

"A truer statement was never uttered," stated Ivara as she ran her clawed hands through her tightly curled hair. "Even The Luck can't resist my wily charms," she finished, referring to Vanidor by one of his other monikers, and eliciting laughter from her companions.

The group rode on for several more hours in a generally northeasterly direction, carrying on a lively conversation that had Cavazos regaling Ferika with tails of their many adventures. More than once, he was interrupted by either Grimlocke or Ivara as they sought to clarify one point or another that the old gnome must have *"accidently"* misstated.

As the day's light started to wane, Cavazos called a

halt to their progress opting to make camp in a small copse of trees that would help provide protection from prying eyes and the cool breeze of the night. As had become their custom over the last few days, Ferika and Cavazos went about setting up the tents, while Ivara and Grimlocke went to round up fire wood, and perhaps catch a hare or two for supper. Ferika enjoyed this part of the journey because it was yet another opportunity for her to grow in her understanding of travel and in fighting tactics. This was because while the food cooked, she was put through martial practice by the three more experienced warriors.

Tonight, Ivara was her sparring partner. Over the last few nights, Ferika had come to learn that Grimlocke used efficient attacks and feints, intended to expend the minimal effort while achieving his desired outcome. Cavazos, perhaps due to his stature and advanced age, relied mostly on a cunning understanding of his opponent's movements and used agility and precise timing to gain an advantage. However, Ivara was a whirlwind of brute strength and blazing speed. Ferika liked sparring with her the most, because although Ivara often left her bruised, the elon was an excellent teacher and seemed to always know what Ferika needed to do to shore up her defenses or launch more effective attacks.

"Don't get lazy, Feri," Ivara hissed, as she noted the slowness with which Ferika was returning her staff to a defensive posture close to her body. "The times after an attack are often when we find ourselves most vulnerable. Focus on keeping your body in balance so that you can quickly revert from offense to defense as the situation calls." The feran elon punctuated this lesson by leaping high into the air to leapt fully over the stunned human, and come down behind Ferika. And even as the girl turned to reacquire her foe, she felt

Ivara's strong arms reach across Ferika's body and yank her backward, flipping her over Ivara's outstretched left leg to fly several feet through the air before landing painfully on the ground.

"I see your point," said Ferika as she scrambled to her feet and swiped her staff at the advancing elon. She must have composed herself more quickly than Ivara had expected as the rushing elon had to jump and twist awkwardly to the side to avoid the sting of Ferika's staff. Agile as a great cat, Ivara landed on her feet and kicked out her foot aiming for the trailing end of the staff. The force of her kick added to the momentum of Feri's swing causing the teen to take a few quick steps to the right in order to regain her balance.

"There's hope for you yet, Feri," spoke Cavazos as he interrupted the sparring session with steaming bowls of soup that he handed to each of the women. "Grim outdid himself this time," the gnome said as he returned to his place beside the fire and began working his way through the delicious meal."

"Venison, wild onions, potatoes, carrots, a dash of salt and a healthy dose of ground gwarvar, and you got yerself a meal fit for eaten," retorted the dwarf around a spoonful of food.

Ferika hadn't eaten many things prepared with gwarver, but over the last few days she had grown quite fond of the red and purple unterland fruit that was about the size of a small melon and had an oddly satisfying sweet and spicy flavor. She commented once again on how much she enjoyed the Grim's cooking, before stretching her sore muscles and heading for bed.

"Wake me when it is my turn to watch," Ferika muttered before disappearing into her tent.

As she drifted off, the teen overheard smatterings of her companion's conversations and was pleased to hear they seemed genuinely happy to have her along with them. She had known them growing up since Falzadrin, her uncle on her mother's side, used to be a part of their treasure seeking troupe. Falzadrin and the rest came by her village often and would stick around for weeks at a time. Ferika loved hearing their tales of adventure and often wondered what it would be like to have the freedom to strike out on the open road at any time. But this was the first time she actually traveled with the group and she was a bit nervous she would do things wrong and that they would regret having her along. It made her sleepy heart glad to hear their comments and as thunder groaned in the distance her dreams were filled with wonder and adventure.

Two days later, Ferika was not at all enjoying her time on the road. She sat upon her horse, as heavy raindrops fell upon her and worked their way beneath her clothing and armor. She cast her eyes about and saw the others looked equally as miserable in the deluge. The heavy clouds continued to vent their wrath upon the land, buffeting the waterlogged travelers with wave after wave of ponderous rainfall. It had been raining, more on than off, for a day and a half now, and while the travelers would have preferred to sit it out under a makeshift shelter, they had to press on to keep ahead of their pursuers.

A day ago, the group was attacked by a band of minotaurs that had used the cover of the storm to sneak up on their encampment. If it were not for the keen eyes of

Grimlocke, who happened to catch a glimpse of armor in the distance, they probably would not have made it out of the situation alive. However, he and Cavazos confronted the approaching enemy with spells and arrows, to give Ivara and Ferika time to gather their horses and supplies and beat a swift retreat. To their dismay, what they thought would just be four or five minotaurs turned out to be a larger hunting party, with many more members. While the two were able to kill several of their attackers, the rest continued their dogged pursuit of the fleeing adventurers.

"We can't go on like this," spoke Ivara, her voice raised to a loud whisper to be heard above the rain. "We have to find a way to shake them, or to end them," she concluded as her hand rested upon the spear housed within her battle saddle. Although Ivara preferred to fight unarmed, she was proficient with many types of weapons, and wielded a spear with deadly efficacy.

Cavazos spurred their horse to get closer to Grimlocke's horse, before handing Ferika the reins to their brown mare. He looked askance at Ivara, and said "Call on an ally to see if you can find a defensible position in all of this morass." To Grimlocke, the gnome said, "Be in the wind, and see what you can do to slow our pursuers."

"Anything beats running like fear driven gurkas after a sun drake sighting," the dwarf replied as he flexed his powerful wings. Ferika marveled that the dwarf's downy feathers proved fast against the rain as the heavy droplets found no purchase there. Without another word, the dwarf shoved off the horses back and soared into the air, empathically calling his deadly bow to hand and drawing upon the magic of the Shadow Sea to cloak him from sight.

Hopping into the now empty saddle, Cavazos looked

up in time to see a falcon emerge from a nearby tree and streak across the sky, headed in the opposite direction as the dwarf. From the way Ivara's eyes tracked the bird, Cavazos knew she had cast Animal Ally, a minor spell that let the caster see through the eyes of a small creature. To be sure, Ivara had enough understanding of magic to cast more powerful spells, but she liked this one as it did not cause any undue harm to the enspelled animal.

"Stay close, and be ready," Cavazos stated as he loosened the straps anchoring Tempest to his hip. Ferika freed her staff from its bindings on her saddle as her horse followed closely behind the others. A strange kind of excitement tingled within her. She had been on raids with her people, but those were often carried out in large numbers against enemies that had been previously scouted. Here, she found herself amongst a group that was outnumbered, with no real understanding of their foe's capabilities. Minotaurs had a fierce reputation and the teen had never crossed weapons with one. She both dreaded, and looked forward to, the apparently inevitable confrontation that was rapidly approaching.

After what seemed like a lifetime, Ivara's head jerked swiftly to the east, and she whispered, "There. It looks like there is an entrance to a cave up that way. I can't tell how far back the cave may go, but it is better than anything else I have seen around here. If nothing else, it will give us something firm to put at our backs as we face the minotaurs." Although the situation was dire, Ferika could see the glint of anticipatory excitement sparkling in the fierce elon's eyes.

"Lead the way," was all Cavazos said as he conjured a spell to mentally inform Grim of their plans.

Several miles away, Grim winged his way over the terrain. The area was mainly open grassland with few trees to obstruct his view, thus he could see the small mass of minotaurs; half of whom were on horseback. Two of the walking minotaurs held leashed dogs whose noses kept dipping to the ground and scouring the air for the barest trace of their prey's passage. The dwarf knew there was little chance of his party evading this group, even with the constant rainfall that seemed to be impeding the progress of the hounds a bit.

Yet, even as he contemplated his next course of action, one of the minotaurs shouted, "Beware, enemy on the wing," before hurling his spear at the flying dwarf. Caught off guard by the minotaur's recognition of his presence, Grimlocke had to work hard to dodge the expertly aimed missile. Tucking his wings in close, the soaren dwarf allowed himself to fall thirty feet closer to the ground before pulling up and weaving his way through a series of boulders that towered like monoliths among the tall grass. His flight took him to the left of the approaching group and he came up in view ready to let loose with his bow. But, from the way the rest of the minotaurs were furiously casting their gazes to the heavens, Grimlocke assumed his spell had dominated the will of the other minotaurs and only one was able to see him. Quick as he could, Grimlocke scanned the ranks until he found the minotaur that saw through his spell and sent an arrow that screeched like a banshee as it leapt from his bow and found a new home in the left eye socket of the unfortunate foe who had just reacquired his location and was opening his mouth to voice the same to his comrades.

The sudden volume of the enchanted arrow, served its purpose as it caused the group below to devolve into momentary confusion, and thus only two or three of the minotaurs saw the brown-skinned dwarf as he crossed over them, sending down arrow after arrow; each one just as loud as the next. Then, just as suddenly, all was silent as Grim once again called upon the Shadow Sea to conceal his presence.

The dwarf smirked with amusement as he saw most of his arrows had flown true and two more of the minotaurs were off to their eternal rest, while at least three were nursing wounds. However, his merriment was cut short as one of the minotaurs rose into the air, powered by a spell of her own. While she did not appear to be able to see Grimlocke, indicated by her exasperation as her spells to reveal the hidden were unsuccessful, the minotaur was making a circuitous path across the area that would inhibit his attempts to get close enough to do the minotaurs more harm from the air.

Willing his wings to produce no sound, the dwarf quietly landed five feet from a mountain of a minotaur in the rear of the enemy's procession. Opening himself to the Shadow Sea, Grim cast a portal and placed the opening just to his left. He then centered himself and aimed an arrow at the base of the big minotaur's over-thick neck. Letting out a controlled breath, Grim loosed the arrow that silently leapt the short distance, puncturing the minotaur's spine before lodging in his skull. The dwarf let fly four more arrows, including one aimed at the areal minotaur, before stepping into the portal and arriving back at the location from whence he first left his horse. But even as he exited the other side of the portal, Grimlocke grimaced in pain as his hand wrapped around the hilt of a dagger that had been expertly thrown and was now buried deep in his right thigh.

Luckily, I don't need to walk, thought the dwarf as he left the knife in, soared into the sky and followed the mental roadmap to where his friends were holed up.

A few minutes later, Grimlocke landed heavily outside of the cave mouth. Seeing that he was injured, Ferika rushed over to tend to his wound. Ivara registered his presence, but did not cease in her attempt to shore up their makeshift fort. Her muscles bulged under the weight of the large deadfall tree trunk she dragged towards the entrance. Meanwhile, Cavazos was exploring the inside of the cave to see if there was any possibility of them escaping deeper within its depths. He came back just as Ferika was finishing the wrapping of Grim's wound.

"It does seem as if the cave goes deeper into the unterland, but the access would be a tight squeeze for any but myself. And we would have to give up the horses, which is not a prospect I would propose. Hopefully the enemy will lose our trail, although that doesn't seem very likely," said the gnome with a resigned look upon his face.

"Your assessment of the situation is accurate as usual," spoke Grim as he tested his leg by putting weight upon it. When he realized it was sound, he gave an appreciative nod to Ferika before walking into the cave to help calm the horses, and began describing what he had encountered to the rest of the group.

"Okay, the blockage here should give the minotaurs some pause as they are not want to walk head first into an ambush. If you and I," Ivara started, motioning Cavazos, "hide outside and wait until they come close, then we can pick off a few of them, while Grim unleashes Hazar's wrath with those deadly arrows of his. Feri, you can remain inside the cave to back Grim up, should any of the buggers breach the barricade." She finished, smirking at Grim's grimace over her reference to the Goddess of Death, for she knew that was one deity Grim would never pray to.

Ferika did not miss the quick furtive glances the other cast her way, and suddenly it donned on her that this cave was for her protection. The others, more than likely, would have preferred to face such odds out in the open where Grim's wings, Ivara's speed and Cavazos' guile would come in handy. Yet, they had identified her as the weak link in their little adventuring troupe and, as a mother with a child, they sought to protect her as best they could.

"I won't let you down," was all she could say as anger and embarrassment warred within her heart.

"I know you won't, little sister," stated Ivara as she gripped her spear and took a seat on the pile of wood, waiting for the enemy to get closer.

As sounds of the approaching force drew closer, Cavazos and Ivara prepared to stalk out into the growing gloom. Ferika quickly stepped up and placed a hand on both of them. "May Danu's will protect you," she said as she opened herself to the flow of magic and shaped the currents into the spell Pound for Pound, which increased both combatants speed, strength and agility.

Feeling the surge of energy infuse her body, Ivara let out a low feral growl, and whispered, "Time to hunt," before she and Cavazos went to cause harm.

The minotaur at the head of the procession was small, by his race's standards. Standing just under six feet tall with oddly colored deep-orange and gray fur, Taomahk had to work hard to achieve his position of honor amongst his people. For that reason, he was assigned as the personal guard of Tsier, the female leader of this expedition. It was Tsier who had first come across the trail of these interlopers and had ordered that they must be sacrificed, and their magic items confiscated for the glory of Bakarri, Goddess of Darkness.

Taomahk, had thought the group they now followed was too meager a prize to expend so much effort, but he was just a male and acquiesced to the towering Tsier in all matters. But after the brief skirmish with the soaren dwarf, that left several of his comrades dead and saw Tsier take an arrow to the arm, Taomahk was beginning to rethink his assessment of the prey before them. At least one of the enemy's numbers had proven himself to be a worthy foe. If the others, two more they all assumed given the number of horses, were as capable then this would be a kill worth bragging about.

The constant rain had washed away most of the signs of their targets' passage. Where it not for the hounds, Taomahk was sure they would have lost the trail by now. But as the group of minotaurs started up a low incline, headed towards a more heavily wooded section of terrain, he knew the chase would soon be coming to an end. He slowed, allowing other minotaurs to take the lead and placing himself closer to Tsier, who acknowledged him with a nod. Placing one meaty finger to her bovine lips, she indicated that he should not speak. Taomahk assumed she must be communing with the spirits, as was her custom prior to entering combat.

Just as Taomahk was beginning to turn his attention back to the surrounding terrain, Tsier turned her head to the right and released a dazzling stream of necrotic light from her outstretched hand. The sizzling bolt sped across the distance and slammed into the tall grass mere seconds after a large figure leapt into view and rushed two minotaurs that were only then starting to dismount from their horses.

Without hesitation, the brown-skinned behemoth buried her crystalline spear in the throat of the closest minotaur before reversing her momentum to bring the deadly weapon down and then in an upward arc that cleaved through the arm of the second minotaur, almost surgically detaching the appendage at the shoulders. To his credit, the wounded male clubbed at the behemoth with his left hand, but hit only air as the attacker carried on her dash directly across the minotaur line, dodging and weaving several attempts to hit her.

Four minotaurs broke off the main group in pursuit, ignoring the bellowed orders of Tsier, who demanded the group to remain together. The wisdom of her warning was further underscored as a gray-haired gnome, all but invisible within the tall grass, stepped out and slammed his mace into the left knee of the fourth pursuer. The unfortunate creature's roar of agony was drowned out by the deafening sound of thunder as his knee exploded, showering his fellows with meat, bone and sinew. The gnome once again lost himself within the tall grass, but made his presence known moments later as another peal of thunder sounded as he shattered the ankle of the minotaur that had turned to check on the status of his fellow. This one, now prone due to the loss of his foot, looked up to see the grim determination written on the gnome's cherubic face as death accompanied his overhead swing.

After a few tense moments, the other two minotaurs returned to the main group, carrying their wounded comrade to present to Tsier for healing. Understanding that the leg was gone, and angered by the foolishness of their actions, Tsier spat on the maimed beast and said, "Your foolishness led to his disaster. I'll not waste spells because of your stupidity. Leave him, as we conquer this foe. If he survives until our return, then I will see what can be salvaged of him."

Taomahk caught the eyes of several of his fellows and stared a warning to them. In this matter, Tsier's word was inviolate and any hesitation would not be tolerated. The diminutive minotaur tightened his grip on the sword at his waist, but did not have to draw it, since the two dropped their wounded ally and all turned their attention to the matter at hand.

Moving at a more measured pace, the minotaurs were determined not to be caught unawares again. Tsier used her magic to call forth three shadowy specters that she sent out to find her prey. Sounds of battle could be heard a short while later as her shadows engaged one, or both, of their enemies. She ordered her column to move faster to get there while the enemy was occupied. Having seen what the enemy could do, she knew her conjured shadows would cause the enemy any real trouble.

They soon arrived at a spot where the tree cover was a bit thicker and seemed to run up the hill on either side of a small cavemouth, that was partially blocked by wood. About thirty feet in front of the cave, a large female elon was swiping her magnificent spear through the last of the shadows. Seeing the minotaur force arrayed before her, the elon opened her fang-filled mouth and issued a savage growl, that caused the minotaurs hounds to whimper and cower. Taomahk instantly recognized the spear as being made of cataglass. Cataglass was the name given to the clear bones of catawals, mighty predators that stalk grassland and woodland settings. These magic infused bones, harder than steel with half the weight, were used to create all sorts of wondrous items.

"That weapon is mine," shrieked Tsier as her group systematically advanced on the elon.

"Only if you can take it," answered the gnome, holding forth a mace as he casually stepped from behind a tree several paces to the elon's right. "Oh, and by the way, Lightning Storm!" he concluded causing jagged lines of lighting to spring forth from Tempest to bash into the minotaurs so neatly arrayed before him. The heavy rain, coupled with the fact that most of the minotaurs were covered in metal armor, boosted the lightnings impact, leaving four minotaurs dead and five wounded in its wake.

"Oh my, that looks like it hurt," he quipped as the minotaurs broke ranks and charged the two before them, who were hard pressed to keep just ahead of the threatening weapons. So chaotic was the scene, that Taomahk at first did not register the arrows that were streaking out of the cave. It wasn't until the third one struck the upper thigh of a minotaur standing right in front of him, did he notice two others had fallen beneath the barrage.

"Arrows from the cave!" Taomahk yelled as he drew his thick sword hoisted his shield, and charged the wood barricade. He could hear the sounds of at least two more minotaurs behind him, and subtly modulated his speed so they hit the barrier before he did. Sure enough, an arrow streaked out of the opening, clipping the lead minotaur on the shoulder but causing no real harm. The second in line lowered his shield and used his great bulk to ram into the hastily constructed barricade, which groaned and creaked, but did not break. Thinking to buy his allies a bit of time, Taomahk cast the spell Wind Burst, which caused a buffeting wind to issue from his position and beat back any arrows coming their way.

"Good, that," bellowed one of the leading minotaurs in thanks, as he bunched the muscles in his legs and forced an opening in the wood pile. Once inside, the beast rushed the dwarf who had dropped his bow and was drawing his dwarven cleaver. The dwarf was at a distinct disadvantage and probably would have come to some harm, had not the unseen human female stepped forward and angled her staff in such a way that it tangled with the legs of the charging minotaur causing him to stumble right into the descending blade of the gleaming cleaver.

The human female was thrown back into the cave wall as Taomahk's second Wind Burt spell slammed into her. He urged his remaining companion forward to confront the dwarf as he sought to come around to the dwarf's flank. The diminutive minotaur spat a curse as hardened clay wrapped around the dwarf's body, from the Clay Armor spell cast by the human who was just then regaining her footing. Even still, he paid the human little heed as he pressed the attack against the dwarf whom he knew to be a deadly foe. His sword came in high, opposite his ally's blow that went low. The dwarf worked his cleaver and shield furiously to keep the blades from finding a purchase in his flesh and took a few tentative steps back, attempting to angle himself so both foes where in front of him, but the minotaurs made adjustments of their own and kept the dwarf surrounded.

"Don't you dare ignore me!" snarled the enraged female as she swung her staff in a wildly vicious arc that nearly collided with the horns of the Taomahk's comrade, who took a swipe at her with his axe, but dared not lose focus on the dwarf that had already killed a number of his party.

Ferika hastily stepped into the gap created by the adjusting minotaur and had to quickly duck as his axe missed her head by mere inches. But she was now level with Grim, and some of the pressure was eased from the dwarf, who took advantage of the reprieve to launch a series of attacks at the smaller, but more agile minotaur. Taomahk was not happy with the turn of events, but easily blocked each one of the dwarf's strikes. He even managed a smile as he saw his companion's downward axe stroke easily cleave through the wooden staff, which the foolish human tried to use to deflect it.

"Finish her quickly!" he shouted after viewing the spout of blood that appeared from the wound on her shoulder. Eager for the kill, the minotaur let out a bleating sound of pleasure as he rushed after the human that had turned and was running towards the back of the small cave.

Outside of the cave, Ivara was just completing her round about kick, that had a many scarred minotaur falling back with a smashed nose, when she caught a glimpse of the battle within the cave. Her heart sank as she saw Ferika frantically running from an axe wielding minotaur. Anger welled within the elon's heart and she swung her spear in an arc, hoping to create enough distance from her immediate foes so she could rush to the girl's aid. But even as she took her first steps in that direction, she saw Ferika run several steps up the back wall of the cave and then kick off, turning in the air and aiming a shard of her broken staff directly at the heart of her approaching foe. The minotaur following the Ferika belatedly realized his peril and tried to stop short, but his momentum carried him unerringly into the hurtling woman and allowed her weapon to slip easily between the seams of his armor, bringing a sharp pain and then oblivion.

"Nice!" yelled Ivara, before grunting under the impact of a club strike that caused her to stumble several paces before regaining her balance. The elon grimaced the pain away and turned her full attention on the fight at hand only to see Cavazos appear suddenly, leaping off a fallen log to slam Tempest into the back of one of the minotaurs. The gnome then dodged a lazy sword thrust as he ran to stand next to Ivara. Both of them sported open wounds and bruises, but they had given better than they had received, which was evident from the many minotaur corpses that lay strewn around the area.

"The cavalry has arrived," said the gnome who used his innate affinity to the element of earth had paid off once again. As the ground beneath their feet started to rumble, Cavazos shot a wink Ivara's way and motioned for her to start falling back towards the cave.

Ignorant to the cause of the vibrations, the two closest minotaurs began advance only to be impaled by spikes of dirt and gravel that erupted from the ground. This proceeded a large section of the surrounding loam that coalesced into a twenty-foot earth elemental. The mighty creature crushed one minotaur under its bulk as it shot missiles of stone into their ranks, injuring many and causing their horses and hounds to scatter.

No novice to battle, Tsier knew the fight was not going well seeing that her forces had been depleted by more than half. This prey was proving to be tougher than she had anticipated, but the arrival of this lethal elemental was too much. Frustration and shame filled her throat with bile to the point she was barely able to utter the hated words, "Retreat,

retreat! Arguent, Begloth, go after those horses, the rest of you to me. Concentrate your attacks on the elemental and head back down the hill."

The surprise of hearing Tsier run from a battle nearly cost Taomahk his life as he nearly missed the sneaky underhand swipe of the dwarf's cleaver. Twisting far to the right, the unbalanced minotaur gave up ground to the advancing threat. Once again focused on matters at hand, Taomahk blocked a descending blow, sending the dwarf's arm out wide. With both of their weapons out of position, the minotaur kicked the dwarf's shield hard, sending his sturdy foe to the ground. Instead of taking advantage of the opening, Taomahk quickly raised his left hand to the pendant on his neck and teleported away.

The sound of an axe hitting the cave wall came about a second after the minotaur's retreat. Grimlocke followed the trajectory of the thrown weapon in time to see Ferika grimace in frustration and say, "By Fa'al's flickering light, I almost had him." Feri's reference to the God of Fate, elicited a laugh from the dwarf as he stood up to survey the damage.

"Looks like we won the day," said the bleeding dwarf as his bruised and battered companions joined them in the cave.

"Things didn't go as smoothly as I would have liked," responded Ivara who went to retrieve a waterskin from one of the horses. "Thank The Luck for giving Cavazos an affinity for the element of earth. If it weren't for our large friend out there," she continued, pointing to the marauding elemental, "we would probably still be fighting."

"All part of a day's work," smirked the exhausted gnome, who gladly accepted the proffered waterskin. The gnome drank deeply before slouching heavily against the wall. He watched as Ferika made the rounds cleaning and bandaging minor injuries, while casting healing spells to close more serious wounds. The young Keltan had learned well from the Society of Alms (a faction known for its healing ways) and Cavazos again thought about how nice it was to have Feri along for the ride.

Chapter 8:
UNDERSTANDING

The slow-moving caravan of over forty wagons left the grasslands and headed into the forested northeastern region of the Archstone Range. Z'har gave the neck of his borrowed horse a gentle rub as he looked back at the advancing wagons. He wondered why Sherkzin opted to push on into the growing gloom, but figured the young dwarf knew what she was doing. Over the last few days, the raven-haired shield dwarf had proved herself as a skilled leader. It was clear she had the respect of the merchants as well as the twenty-four mercenaries hired to protect them. Each day, Sherkzin made a point to stop by each of the wagons to check on her charges and to update them on the course of the day's journey. Such attentiveness was natural for dwarves, but was uncommon amongst the many caravan leaders Z'har had encountered over the years.

The good will Sherkzin had engendered amongst the guards, most of whom had worked for her more than once, was put to the test a few days back when she informed the caravan Z'har and Niska would be tagging along for a bit of the journey. While none bulked at the inclusion of the female burvore, more than a few muffled complaints could be heard about having a gods cursed pointy-ear in their midst. Sherkzin always encouraged her people to speak their minds, and listened patiently as two of her guards did just that. One, a short-statured human female with blonde hair, an eyepatch and a strong Keltan accent said the only use she ever had for elves was as target practice. While a long-limbed shorn with bulbous eyes and thick head frills added elves also made fine ingredients in tree-hugger stew.

Though a consummate diplomat, Sherkzin would not broker such insensitive and callous talk and quickly put the two in their place, explaining if their hearts were so set on the matter then she had no further use for them. She dismissed them on the spot, then just as quickly returned to her conversation with the rest of the guards that ultimately culminated in most of them grudgingly agreeing to accept the pair. Others kept their thoughts to themselves. Judging by the stares Z'har (who was standing no more than fifty paces away) received understood the bulk of the guards were not happy, but would acquiesce to the dwarf's judgement.

The conversation with the merchant owners of the wagons went pretty much the same way, although more were swayed by the potential profit this caravan trip could bring them, and were willing to overlook the low-born character of one of the guards. All in all, things went smoother than Z'har had expected, but even though Sherkzin said he did not have to, the elf felt it was better for him to ride ahead of the caravan each day. He told Sherkzin and Niska it was the least he could do as a way to earn his keep along the journey, but Niska new (and Sherkzin suspected) it was easier for the elf to brave the dangers of the road than to deal with the pervasive prejudice that faced him on a daily basis.

In contrast to Z'har's self-imposed isolation, Niska made herself right at home amongst the guards and often traveled with one or two fellows as they exchanged positions up and down the length of the caravan. The burvore's easy going nature, and great story telling ability allowed her to quickly insinuate herself in many situations. Each night, she held sway around the campfire riveting guards and merchants alike with tales of combat and mischief. Most of the stories she told were directly from their own experiences and though Z'har knew the outcome, he found himself drawn into the lyricism of the burvore's cadence and was just as enthralled as the other listeners.

Thinking of the absurdity of it all, Z'har chuckled to himself as he let out a calming breath and pushed further ahead into the woods. "So, our lone defender can find joy in his heart," came a voice as Sherkzin appeared out of the gloom, atop her massive black stallion.

The surprised elf was no stranger to scouting and knew the value of stealth, but had never before encountered anyone that could match this young dwarf when it came to moving without detection. His face clouded in a scowl as he chided himself for being caught so completely flatfooted. He kept his eyes on the road ahead as he responded, "If I am indeed this caravan's lone defense than I wonder about our prospects given the way you so easily unarmed my senses."

"Oh, think nothing of it, little elf," Sherkzin quipped as she brought her mount parallel to his. "Blackstar and I have had a bit more… training in the quiet arts, then most can boast of." At the mention of his name, the dwarf's horse made a noise that was reminiscent of a human's snicker, and Z'har inferred once again there was more than meets the eye when it came to that magnificent steed.

"Speaking of boasting," the dwarf continued in a jovial tone, "Niska is back there spinning quite a doozy of a tale. What's all this about you rescuing a band of adventurers from a handful of thieves including a mage and her pet swamp giant? The way she tells it, that blade of yours and your two mysterious hounds made short work of those dread baddies."

"While the tail is mostly true," Z'har said, feeling his face flush with embarrassment, "I'm sure Niska makes it out to be far grander than it was. You know Niska and I left the valley to find the girl from my dream walks. Well, we had been in the Archstone Range for about a tenday when we heard rumors a girl had been kidnapped. While we didn't think it was the same girl, it was at least worth a look. After some time, we learned the full tale of events and realized it was not at all connected to our mission. However, by then we were invested in the outcome and had planned to follow the trail to its conclusion."

There he stopped, intending to say no more, but Sherkzin's silence, and her imploring eyes, loosened his tongue and the elf found himself continuing. "We had heard about a group of natals that were deep into the whole human sacrifices thing, and were on our way to disrupt their plans, when we heard sounds of battle behind a lone outpost. It appears as if the thieves had laid a trap for the adventurers, who were clearly out of their depth. By the time we showed up, the whole place was ringed in fire and the giant was stalking in for the kill. We intervened, and while I did tussle with the giant, it was Bodica and Zion that really took the fight to him, but I must admit it was quite a scrap."

Z'har paused as he let the events of that day play out in his mind, before saying, "Anyway, after the fight, we learned the group was actually hired by the girl's village to affect her rescue and thus left the matter in their hands. I don't know how that situation played out, but I felt pretty good about their odds." By the time he finished his retelling, Z'har was smiling in spite of himself.

"She's a smart one, that burvore friend of yours," Sherkzin said after digesting the whole of the tale. "She knows one of the best ways to change the hearts and minds of people is just for them to be exposed to stories and concepts they would not have previously considered and go against their ignorant assumptions. It is a sad fact that it is often more effective for one that is accepted to advocate for the shunned, then for the shunned to do so themselves."

Z'har pondered her words and could only shake his head in agreement as he realized his friend was doing just that. "I never looked at it that way," he admitted. "I just assumed Niska was being her friendly old self."

"I'd wager there is a bit of that in there too," replied Sherkzin, "But I have seen the way people hang on her every word, as if they themselves are taking part of some grand adventure, which just so happens to put you on the side of the just more times than not. That kind of thing has a way of sinking into one's psyche just as thoroughly as messages received by negative stereotypes. Most people hate other people because they have learned to do so. I've never witnessed a child born with hatred in their heart; at least not a child that wasn't an infernal being," she finished, referencing the group of extraplanar creatures that encompassed races such as demons, devils and ashanas.

"I'm sure you are right. Within the Valley of Shale, I was sheltered from the reality of the hatred for my people that is so wide spread. The residents of Skyfall held true to a doctrine that individuals should be judged by their actions and not by some arbitrary aspect such as the race they were born into." Z'har stated as he looked back on his years within the valley. While not the most common races, Z'har knew that Skyfall boasted of having hobgoblins, brawns, hroshims and even a smattering of orcs amongst their citizenry. He even recalled seeing an elf or two over the years. "I was ill prepared for what I would face beyond the valley's high walls," he confessed.

"I know of the teachings of Olorun, for he is an honored ancestral spirit. I suspect the elders hate the treatment of your people and probably sought to shield you from the hurt of it. That is probably why they did not craft a mask for you to wear when outside of their enclave. After all, it's not as if they expected you to go traipsing too far beyond the walls of Skyfall. But their judgement was flawed and has left you disarmed in the face of such a nefarious foe," Sherkzin said as she locked eyes with the young elf. "But know that I do not share such abhorrent beliefs and you will ever have a place within my caravan."

"My thanks," answered Z'har who broke eye contact to stare into the growing darkness. "To be honest, I didn't hear many stories of elves as I was growing up. I had heard elves mostly exist in myth as few have ever seen one, and when they are seen they always have a mask covering their face. Radelerz Dekalbite, the commander of the Sky Guard, offered to have a mask crafted for me to wear when out on patrols, but I thought it was more honorable to show my face to illustrate I have nothing to hide …and they have nothing to fear.

"I have seen your face and am starting to get some since of the heft of your heart. I pray Bran's protection over you and your loyal friend as your road leads you beyond my reach." Sherkzin said, before turning her horse in the direction of the following caravan. "I guess I have held your ear long enough. We will follow this path for another hour or two. It will lead us to a safehold where we will camp for the next two nights. I don't anticipate any trouble between now and then, but you never know. At any rate," she continued as she cast one last meaningful look at Z'har, "I do expect to see you around the campfire tonight. It will do my heart well to see you enjoying a meal with future-companions. Have faith my friend."

Z'har heard the dwarf's parting words but did not respond. The thought of sitting with the mixed group of merchants and guards while they supped around a big bonfire filled him with an anxiety that he did not wish to contemplate at the moment. Instead, he tried to focus on the sound of Sherkzin's leaving. But try as he might, the elf could not hear more than two or three footfalls of Blackstar and then… nothing. Z'har's eyes seemed to glow as they reflected the waning light but even with his starsight, the elf could register no trace of the dwarf.

Z'har was familiar with the concept of safeholds; small fortified structures maintained by local authorities to be used as bastions of safety for travelers along the open road. But the one he now approached felt more like a miniature fort, than a site designed for brief layovers. Ten-foot stone and wood walls surrounded a large courtyard that housed a large stone building and a smaller wooden outbuilding. While the safehold could not house all of the caravan's wagons, there was ample room for the merchants to haul their most valuable merchandise within the safety of the walls. The wagons were arranged in three orderly rows, running horizontally in front of the compound. The height of the walls gave the guards a clear line of sight in all directions.

After completing their turn on the wall, Z'har slowly followed Niska as they wound their way through a throng of tents to sit on one of the long logs arranged around the courtyard's large fire pit. The sounds of conversation and laughter could be heard from the main building, where some of the haughtier merchants opted to spend their time. Silence reigned for the moment at the bonfire as merchants and guards focused their attention on the savory meal of shaved duck, cheese bread and mashed beans. Most of the people chased their meal with warm ale or spiced milk, but Niska and Z'har opted for the berry fusion brewed by a halfling merchant with dazzling hazel eyes and an odd shaped purplish birthmark on the left side of her face.

Z'har felt a brief pat on his shoulder and turned to see Sherkzin walking by to get a plate of her own. The dwarf took a seat at the fire and was soon engrossed in one of the many lively conversations that sprang up. Z'har tried his best to appear relaxed and engaged, but could feel his pulse rising as he considered what questions might be asked of him and what his responses would be. Luckily only one or two questions or comments came his way, and the elf was able to sit in relative obscurity listening to the others. He couldn't understand why he felt this way as he had no trouble carrying on conversations in small settings, or even when addressing large audiences on matters of conflict and the like. But the thought of carrying out casual conversations, while suspecting that many people here held his race in such low regard, was almost more than he could bear.

"…and that's when Z'har here," said Niska, placing her hand on her friend's arm and drawing him back to the here-and-now, "takes that pig-sticker of his and practically decapitates the zama. The Luck was with him since that was when the boulder I loosened finally fell and closed off the tunnel, sealing the rest of them in."

"Is that the truth of it, poi… uh, elf?" asked Fildmog, one of the guards stated, barely beating back her use of the racial slur.

All eyes turned to Z'har, who would rather have been anywhere else at the moment. "It is as she said," stated the elf, working hard to keep the nervousness out of his voice. "Although as I recall, the boulder was much larger and the zama much smaller than in my friend's retelling."

"Always so modest," interjected Sherkzin with a laugh. "You see, this is why I asked these two to join us for a bit. They were raised under the tutelage of my cousin, Mihoko Nurak, and she don't train em weak. By Demmis' fiery furnace, I've only ever lost two merchants while running caravans and that was way back nearly twenty years ago when I first started out. I don't intend to ever lose a third, and know how to find good protection for my charges. Heck, there was this one time about six or so years back, when we ran up against a whole mess of andronу. Now, I don't know what them bug folks was doing in these parts, but…" the dwarf continued, as relief filled Z'har and the elf used that moment to excuse himself from the group.

About twenty minutes later, Niska entered the tent and filled Z'har in on the conversations he missed. She could sense the turmoil within her dear friend and knew he would open up when he was ready. Instead, she pulled out the vial provided by Sunziprix and made sure Z'har had a dose of the draught to ensure he had a peaceful night's rest.

Niska awoke the next morning and sat in silence as Z'har finished his meditation. She and the elf then grabbed some breakfast before going to wash in a nearby stream. The clean, crisp water washed away the last dregs of sleep from their bodies and left them both invigorated.

"Up for some training," Z'har asked.

"Always," Niska said, as she crossed the stream and headed deeper into the woods.

While it was not uncommon to see the guards, and even some of the merchants, going through sparring routines in the early morning, or in the coolness of the evening air, Niska and Z'har did not join in. This was partially over concerns that someone might let their unfounded hatred of elves turn what should be a practice session into a real fight. But mainly it was because they needed a space, away from prying eyes, if they were going to truly practice, which meant employing their zin abilities. This was mainly a concern for Niska, as Z'har's abilities (other than his enhanced healing) were not readily apparent. However, one of Niska's abilities was to create and manipulate objects by siphoning energy and material from the surrounding elements. Not too many people would miss her conjuring a twenty-foot spike that shot from the ground to impale a nearby tree.

"That was a close one," toyed Z'har as he easily avoided that very missile. He tapped it with his sword, then did a mock bow, before sending a wink Niska's way.

"Well, that's only cause you're part monkey," she

smirked, referring to the superior agility afforded by his zin ability to instantly adapt to nearly any situation. "Why, I bet if I were to conjure up a river and dump it on you, you'd sprout gills and simply float away," she finished with a laugh as the vine she conjured out of the tall grass snaked around the tree and grabbed hold of the unsuspecting elf's sword arm.

"What's this now," quipped Z'har as he rotated his wrist, easily slicing the vein asunder. But that brief distraction was all that Niska needed to close the gap between them and barrage the elf with strikes and feints utilizing her dagger and sword. Z'har's smile disappeared as he worked to keep Niska's weapons at bay, and looked for that one opening, which came as Niska made a bold double thrust towards his abdomen that would have skewered a lesser opponent, but Z'har was no regular combatant. Seeing the burvore's attack as if in slow motion, Z'har lowered his blade and shield in an X motion, blocking the weapons towards the ground while summersaulting over the burvore to rest his sword against the nape of her exposed neck.

"I guess I overplayed that last strike," Niska said, conceding the fight was lost to her. The burvore sheathed her sword and walked over to take a seat at the base of a wide tree. She toyed with her dagger and looked up at her older brother, as her thoughts traveled to what they had witnessed in the dream walk. The two had spoken of it several times since that day, and while both felt saddened by seeing the demise of their parent, it only served as confirmation of what they had feared for quite a while. After all, it was not within the character of Borack and Winchunset to abandoned their adopted children. All of the Fallowsheirs had accepted long ago that they may never see their parents again, but the truth of how they died left more questions than it answered.

"I know what we saw," Niska continued, her voice barely above a whisper, "but it just doesn't make any sense."

"I get it," Z'har replied as he slumped down heavily beside her. As the eldest of the Fallowsheirs he felt as if he always had to be strong for his younger siblings, but somehow Niska saw through his facade of strength and always figured out a way to coax out his inner thoughts. It was yet another reason why Z'har felt so close to his little sister and dearest friend. "I keep thinking of the look on dad's face as he realized that Anguta was calling him home," he said referencing the Goddess of Disruption, also known as the Seraph of Death. "Worse still, what must he have thought to know that is was the love of his life that was sending him down the Lonely Road?"

"I don't understand, what could have made mom turn on him like that? Who is this Serafeen person mom mentioned to the mongruul vamps she traveled with? And where were the hounds?" Niska continued unconsciously lowering her eyes to Z'har's chest that now bore the enchanted tattoo through which Bodica and Zion gained entrance into this world.

"Maybe dad had sent them away before mom… before mom attacked him. Or maybe they were busy fighting the other vampires," the elf said, struggling for rationality out of the chaos of his emotions. "As for Serafeen, I'm sure that answer awaits along the path we now tread."

"So, you do think she was a vampire?" Niska asked, noting his use of the word, other, though deep down she already knew the answer. The two had been taught enough lore about those dangerous creatures to know one when they saw it. "How… When did she become a vampire? And who is this Serafeen person that she spoke of?"

Bereft of answers, Z'har sat in silence before responding. "It looks like this mission keeps getting more complicated with each step we take. The only thing that I do know for sure is Leloni was supposed to be our newest sister, and that for some reason, I am either destined to be her savior or her murderer."

"Whoa," interjected Niska, not willing to concede that the brother she loved so much would take the life of an innocent. "That is wrong! Yes, she was to be a Fallowsheir, but that last part is not clear. I don't believe you would do that, and I don't think you believe it either." Here, Niska scooted closer to her brother, her friend, and gently turned his face towards hers. "Search your heart, Z'har. Do you bear her any ill will? Do you think that you could… that you will bring her harm?"

"No," was the word that leapt out of Z'har's mouth. He told himself he felt nothing but sorrow for the child, yet doubt festered like a coiled snake deep within his heart. "But then again, if you would have asked me if mom would ever turn on dad, I would have said the same thing… no. And look how that turned out."

"So, what you're saying is I just have to make sure you don't get turned into a vampire," smirked Niska, trying to interject some humor into the situation. "That should be a pretty easy task, except we're apparently headed straight towards someone that does business with those Demmis-spawned bloodsuckers."

"Always looking on the bright side," Z'har quipped, willing lightness into his heavy heart. He knew the road ahead was uncertain and all of their questions would be answered in time. He was just not sure he was ready for the answers they might find. He painted a half-hearted smile on his face and began to stand up.

"I was going for…" the burvore's words trailed off as her sensitive ears detected movement in the woods to her right." From the way Z'har's elongated ears swiveled in that direction, she could tell he had heard it too.

The pair quietly crept in the direction of the noise, and were unnerved to see a large contingent of minotaurs headed in the direction of the safehold. Niska's initial thought was to rush back to the compound to alert the others of the coming force, but he then remembered that eagle-eyed Estrovan, the lone drek guard, was one of the ones on watch. Couple that with the fact Rettuc had set out to patrol the area on his winged alicorn, Serutac, and she was sure the camp was already aware of the approaching danger.

She caught Z'har's eye and sent him a questioning glance. He must have been thinking along the same lines as her since he motioned his hand in the direction of the approaching force. Niska chose a path through the woods that allowed them to circumnavigate the minotaurs who were making no attempt to hide their approach. She was stunned to see how large the force was when she counted ten heavily armored brutes walking ahead of thirty minotaurs on horseback. The whole procession was followed by six covered wagons with ten more minotaurs covering the rear. The seasoned duo had no trouble evading the notice of the minotaur's scouts and soon identified the leader of the force. At the forefront of the horse riders was a female minotaur with scarlet armor and a missing horn. Her bulk was impressive, even for a minotaur and Niska silently thought that she'd let one of the hounds handle that one.

Not wishing to tip their hand too soon, the pair shadowed the minotaur procession until it came to a halt about sixty feet from the stronghold's walls. She was surprised to see the gate of the compound was still open, and that the guards on the wall seemed to be at ease. Before long, Sherkzin road out to meet the minotaur leader, who greeted her with a firm arm clasp. The burvore was too far away to hear their words, but surmised from their mannerisms the pair were known to each other, if not outright friends.

"Fear not, my friends," came Sherkzin's voice in their heads, sending her thoughts by way of a spell, even as she carried on a conversation with the minotaur's leader. "These are not enemies, but are the first of our trading partners along the route. You did well in tracking them, but your deadly skills will not be needed this day. It is perhaps best that you two remain undetected until you are safely within the safehold. I would hate for the hasty actions of one of these guests to lead to bloodshed."

The greetings concluded with the large minotaur gesturing to her group who began to spread out and set camp. Niska and Z'har used their distraction to make their way cautiously back to the safehold, and were soon sipping a strawberry fusion as the merchants streamed out of the safehold anxious to show their wares and hopefully find a bargain amongst the provisions brought by the minotaurs who were known for their acquisition of unique spices, rich furs and exotic meats.

Later that afternoon, Reveln the minotaur leader, invited Sherkzin and the merchants to dine with her. The dwarf graciously accepted and asked Z'har and Niska to be a part of her four-member honor guard, a mostly ceremonial show of protection that mimicked the practice of many local nobility. As the caravanners made their way across the short distance from the safehold to the prepared eating area, many minotaurs bulked at seeing an elf, and more than a few spat at the ground or muttered curses proclaiming the general awfulness of elves. Sherkzin paid these insults no heed, and Z'har did his best to ignore them as well. But he did not miss as Niska stepped closer to her friend and stared daggers at those that showed their ignorance.

The procession soon arrived at the designated eating area. Before them were two rows of four tables running parallel to the safehold, with a large table set perpendicular to the rest about ten feet away. Z'har guessed the tables must have been carted within one of the wagons and reassembled for an occasion such as this. Reveln stood from her spot at the center of the lone table and was immediately followed by the other two minotaurs sitting at her table, and the eight spread out amongst the other tables.

"I am glad you have graced us with your presence," the minotaur said in passable Dwarf Tongue. "I would be honored if you and your seconds will dine at my table," this last part was spoken in Oromo, which was the most common language spoken amongst the merchant class.

Sherkzin motioned for the honor guard to attend her and the four merchants that moved to Reveln's table. The remaining merchants took seats around the other tables. Z'har did not miss the look in Reveln's eyes or the slight flare of her nostrils at the sight of the elf. She had already been informed of Z'har's presence during their earlier conversation, but had not expected to actually see the elf. Truth be told, she was more curious than disgusted as she had never before seen an elf. A few seats away from Reveln, a male minotaur with a golden nose ring scoffed as the elf drew near and spat out an invective in Mud Tongue, which Z'har roughly understood to mean, "One who sleeps with dirt."

Laughter rippled through the ranks of the minotaurs as the male had expressed what many of them were thinking. But a completely different type of eruption came from Reveln who blurred into motion as she leapt from her seat and grabbed the male by the scruff of his neck.

"You dare insult my guests!" she yelled in Oromo before repeatedly bashing the males head into the stout table until he lost consciousness. "Apologies for the rudeness of this one's behavior," Reveln continued as she kicked the oblivious minotaur out of his seat and motioned for two of her guards to drag him away. "He will be dealt with, and I apparently now have to find someone to share my bed tonight. If that elfling weren't so scrawny, I might give him a whirl." she smirked, seamlessly slipping back into the festive mood of the occasion.

If Sherkzin was put off by the exchange, she did not show it. She laid a comforting hand on Z'har's arm and smiled amiably as she took the proffered seat to Reveln's left. "I thank you for your courtesy," she replied, "and trust all will be as friends this evening, though in truth I'm not sure my elven friend here could manage the passions of what of your stature."

Much of the tension of the moment drained away as the two leaders made light of the recent unpleasantness, completed their formal greetings, and began to converse naturally over the sumptuous meal. Niska, standing several paces behind Sherkzin's chair, was happy that the dwarf had encouraged her and the other honor guard members to eat a stout supper before attending this event. Otherwise, she would be miserable with hunger. Even still, her mouth began to water as the smell of mushroom roasted pig, smoked venison, glazed yams, salted watermelon and much more tickled the danced amongst the sensitive hairs of her nostrils. She glanced at Z'har, who was staring straight ahead, and for all she knew his mind was probably a million leagues away.

How long is this thing going to last? Niska thought to herself for the third time. The afternoon sun had begun to wane as evening arose to take its place. Full meal or no, Niska was having a hard time keeping her eyes off of the stacks of food still heaped around the table. But she quickly snapped back to her senses as a messenger came up to Reveln and bowed apologetically before whispering a message in her ear. While, the burvore was not able to make out all of what was said, she did hear something to the effect about Tsier returning and a great elemental.

Reveln looked at the messenger and then followed his gaze across the row of tables to come to stop on a group of minotaurs standing beside one of the tents. The female minotaur at the head of the smaller group looked disheveled and many of her followers, save for a small male with a dazzling-looking sword and shield, were covered in wounds and shame. Niska was always a bit nosy and her curiosity was surely peaked by the appearance of this other group of minotaurs. However, Reveln apologized to Sherkzin as her attention was needed elsewhere. The dwarf thanked the minotaur for her hospitality and stood. She began walking back towards the safehold, accompanied by her honor guard and soon by all of the merchants as they too recognize the night's festivities had come to an end.

Chapter 9:
Swag

"Pick up the speed on that right hand," Ivara instructed as her stick easily slipped passed Ferika's parry attempt to score a hard hit on the teens exposed torso. She then angled a strike at Feri's head with the stick in her right hand, but that one was blocked cleanly by the youth whose face was a mask of determined concentration.

"Very good," prompted the large elon as Feri pressed forward with a series of strikes from her two sticks. Starting low, the youth worked her weapons up the elon's frame, jarred by the vibrations as each of her attempts were stymied by the Ivara's defense. But when both combatants had their arms up high, Ferika swiftly reversed, bringing her weapons in a backward arc on either side of her body to come together in a double thrust aimed at the elon's stomach.

The crafty attack would have succeeded where it not for the speedy reaction of Ivara who leapt into a backward flip, kicking Feri's hands up high, before landing several feet beyond the teen's reach.

"You nearly caught me with that last trick," Ivara said. She then took up another fighting stance and rushed in to confront her adversary once more.

Ferika worked hard to keep up with the speed and ferocity of Ivara's attacks. As a Keltan, she was no stranger to combat training, and had been in a few dangerous scraps over her fifteen years. However, the events of the last few days had shown her that there was much more to warfare than she was used to. She still had moments of near panic when thoughts of her near-death experience within the cave threatened to overwhelm her. Where it not for her last-minute inspiration to use the wall itself to give her an advantage against her foe, she would now be having her soul weighed by Yen-Lo.

As she attended to the group's wounds following their fight with the minotaurs, she had expressed her fear that she was ill prepared for the road they now tread. The others listened in respectful silence and spoke words of encouragement when she was done.

Cavazos, who had seen over two centuries of life, explained that to live was to learn and since Feri had shown her willingness to live, then they would help her learn and she would do the same for them. The youth's time amongst the Society of Alms had given her a wealth of knowledge regarding anatomy, herb lore, and wound care. Unless the need was dire, they would forgo healing through potions or via a spell and allow Ferika to administer aid. Observing her would increase their collective understanding of how to care for the injured in a variety of circumstances. At the same time, they would take every opportunity to hone her skill at fighting as well as her understanding of the broader world. Each day, when they stopped for camp, Feri's training would begin.

From Grimlocke, she learned the use of the bow, a

weapon seen as cowardly amongst her people. Though she had misgivings about the weapon, she endured the hour-long practice and began to evidence some small aptitude with the weapon.

Ferika would then spend the next hour studying with Cavazos. The gnome produced several books on magic, monsters and obscure lore. He would have the youth read a given passage and then they would discuss what she had learned and how that fit into the broader pattern of life.

Lastly, she would spend an hour of training with Ivara. Since Feri's quarterstaff was cut in two, Ivara found four long slender sticks in the surrounding woods. Having had some training in escrima, a martial art that originated from a place far to the east, she began instructing Ferika in stick fighting. The teen found this hour to be the hardest as she was not ambidextrous as was Ivara. While fighting with a quarterstaff did encourage her to utilize both hands for defense and attacks, the coordination needed for stick fighting was on a completely different level since the attacks came with both hands and often from different angles and speeds. Being left-handed, Ferika had to work hard to improve the strength and control of her right hand. Worse still, was Ivara's belief that pain was a good motivator. Though the elon no doubt held back, her blows were still stinging and often left Ivara bruised.

"Dinner's on," called Grim as he sat by the fire, and repositioned the annul cube to the center of their camp. Ferika had heard of annul cubes before, but had never actually seen one. They were reportedly a staple of forces that relied on stealth and subterfuge during battle. But since the Keltans preferred to fight out in the open, such items were not common amongst her people. From what she understood, annul cubes were devices that concealed sound and light from a given area by blending it with the surroundings so that observers can't discern the true source of the same.

"If my memory serves, there should be a small village within a day's journey of where we are," said Cavazos as he scooped some of the stew into his bowl and took a seat near the fire. "As long as we can continue to elude the various war parties we have seen lately, then we should be able to sup in an actual inn tomorrow."

"Let's hope they have a good bathhouse," quipped Ferika who was more focused on rubbing the soreness out of her muscles than she was on the meal before her. "I could use a nice long hot soak."

"Bah, a little pain is good for you," responded Ivara, pointing to the welt on her leg caused by one of the few times Feri was able to land as solid blow on her. The group spent the next few minutes in conversation as they consumed their meal. As was typical, Ivara took the first watch as the others scampered into their bedrolls and were soon fast asleep.

A few hours past midday, the group came within sight of a walled village. Cavazos could not remember the name of this small hamlet, as he had only been by this way a few times. But he did recall the people were a friendly sort and figured the stop would give them time to resupply, purchase some replacement weapons for Ferika and to get some information about their route ahead.

Grimlocke led the way as the group approached the village. The dwarf nodded to himself as he examined the tall earthen walls; his keen eye picking out weaknesses in the community's defenses. Unlike some larger cities, the group was not asked to peace-tie their weapons. In fact, they were able to enter the village, which they learned was named Mangohal, without much discussion.

The dwarf figured the village must have been visited recently by a mage or two, given the freshness of the runes inscribed on the inside of the dirt wall. He knew enough of magical glyphs to know these runes likely enhanced the durability of the walls to that akin to stone. He took a moment to watch as an elderly lady in long brown robes painted the runes with what appeared to be blood. Grimlocke adjusted his estimation of the wall's strength as he considered the blood was perhaps a payment to local spirits that also added their strength to the village's protection.

The village consisted of perhaps thirty structures, with its only inn located relatively close to the walls. The Green Rest was a cozy looking two story building of wood and stone construction with a thatched roof and a polished oak sign that proclaimed its name in Wood Tongue. As they stepped inside, a kind faced elderly human with faded blonde hair and overly large cheeks introduced herself as Eow, the establishment's owner. She ordered two young boys to attend to their horses and showed them to a table near the hearth.

Happy to be off the open road, the group relaxed into the chairs and enjoyed a meal of fried eggs, sausage and honey-bread, with two pitchers of cinnamon spiced milk. Grim was the first to finish and walked around the room conversing with several of the inn's other patrons. Dwarves were seen as one of the most honorable races of Mythandria and were trusted in nearly all situations. As such, it was not hard for the winged fellow to loosen the tongues of those nearby.

After a time, Grim came back to the table with the others. He had already secured two rooms for the night and explained most of the other patrons were merchants traveling to the larger cities of the Archstone Range to hock their wares. When asked about the warbands he and the others had encountered, most had little to say except it appeared yet another would-be-king has risen in the Outlands somewhere further to the east and is trying to carve out a kingdom through blade and blood. This new threat, Zendrick something-or-other lead a bunch of rowdies calling themselves the Dagba Warriors. While they were a menace, the people that lived on the border between the Archstone Range and the Outlands were a hardy bunch and gave as good as they got. Still, this Zendrick is a persistent sort, and is rumored to be in league with dark creatures from the abyss of Demmis.

"Great," remarked Ivara with a mock frown on her face, "so let me get this straight, we have to go to some far-off frontier town to learn the whereabouts of some mysterious half-elven child in the hopes of rescuing her, while also trying to avoid a maniac and his demonic horde." She paused and stretched her long lean arms before breaking into a radiant smile, "Sounds like just another Nabysday to me," she concluded, making a reference to the second day of a tenday period.

"I know, right?" replied Cavazos with a sparkle in his eye. He did love adventuring so. "Just another baddie in need of some serious attitude adjustment. Avoid em if we can," he started.

"Put em down if we can't," came the unified response as Grim and Ivara added their voice to the party's motto regarding dangerous foes.

"Yeah, we're gonna need to get you some new weapons," Ivara said talking to Ferika.

"Already on it," Grimlocke interjected as his mind switched to business mode. "This village has only one place that sells combat equipment. It's a place called Striker's Choice. The owner, FeldLeeh Bottomswall is reportedly a decent sort that sells quality wares for a fair price. None are too sure about how the halfling procures his stock, but somehow, he always seems to have just what a person is looking for. Why don't you take the youngin to go get her kitted up, and I'll take the old man here and replenish our supplies at the Bag & Wheel."

"Careful who you call old man, you darned winged furball," laughed Cavazos as he patted the mace at his waist. "Tempest has life enough for the both of us and she'll be splitting yer wig ifn ye throw another insult me way," concluded the gnome doing his best imitation of the tired tropes regarding the speech patterns of dwarves.

"I was going to object to youngin," began Ferika. "But since you put it that way, I think I'll just ditto that remark," she finished and put her arm around the gnome's shoulders.

"Consider me forewarned and chastened," Grim said as he stood and dipped into a low bow. "Ivara, would you escort this age-challenged lass as she secures a lance worthy of her ego. As for myself, I will travel with this ancient of days to procure means for our traveling ways?"

"You sir are a true scholar, and a gentleman. It shall be as you have requested," countered Ivara in the manner of the nobility. She then stood and presented her arm for Ferika to take.

"You got jokes," said Ferika who could think of nothing witty to say, and simply laughed as she stood and accepted Ivara's hand with a courtly curtsey.

"You win this round, you sky hopping hippie," Cavazos acknowledged as he stood and headed for the door, tossing a grin and a gold piece at the serving lad that came to clean their table.

The sky was just beginning to take on the glow of morning as the companions made their way out of Mangohal. Their supplies were newly replenished and they all had had a restful night's sleep. Cavazos woke them early so they could make the most of the day's light.

As the troupe resumed their journey, Ferika took out her new weapons in order to get use to their weight in her hands. Striker's Choice did not have any quarterstaff nor any wooden fighting sticks, but true to his reputation, Feld-Leeh Bottomswall did not disappoint. The halfling just so happened to have two metal rods with a comfortable leather hand grips and delicate runes inscribed up their lengths. The halfling said he could not recall how the weapons came into his possession, but was sure they were intended for the young Keltan. Ivara cast Arcane Insight on the metal fighting sticks, and was able to discern they were indeed enchanted. However, she was unable to determine the nature of their magic. Regardless, their worth was evident to Ferika who felt drawn to them as if she was meant to have them all along.

Unfortunately, they were priced far above what the young Keltan could afford. Ivara offered to assist with the purchase, and even took over negotiations with the halfling, who seemed smitten by the dark-skinned beauty. Ferika wasn't sure whether it was the elon's charm or her haggling abilities that finally won out, but either way they walked away with the fighting sticks, a well-made longbow, and two quivers of arrows.

While Ferika was not overly fond of the idea of using ranged weapons, she was determined to improve herself in all areas in order to be more of an asset for the group. Besides, she hoped she could master the bow enough to be able to wound her foes by injuring an arm or leg, taking them out of battle but leaving them alive.

Over the next few days, Ferika pushed herself to her limits, trying hard to master the skills that the others were imparting to her. Sensing the newfound determination of their pupil, the three friends responded by teaching her ever more complex lessons.

Grimlocke moved from their lessons of shooting at a stationary target to hitting a target while on the move, either on foot or from horseback. Ivara found solid wood of varying strengths and used those to get Ferika experience against foes with different fighting styles. This forced Ferika to push her understanding of how to use her new fighting sticks as the attacks came from more angles than she was used to. While she had yet to land a solid blow on Ivara, she was able to block more of the elon's attacks.

Cavazos continued teaching her lore, but also searched his grimoire for healing spells, as well as those that would provide a boost to the team during times of combat. Understanding Ferika's love for her goddess, Danu, the gnome was careful to ensure these spells did not deviate from the will of that deity. Ferika was able to cast some of the spells that she was shown, but not as easily as she would have imagined. The gnome guessed she was attempting to access magic in a way that was foreign to her. Instead of trying to control the flow of magic directly from the Shadow Sea, perhaps she would be better served by achieving the desired spell effect through prayers to Danu. The gnome had little experience with those who performed magic through prayer, rather than actual spells, but believed that was how many of strong religious beliefs did so.

Each night, the teen would crawl into her bedroll, exhausted and sore. But each morning she would rise with a renewed energy and a desire to see what this day would bring. While she missed her home in the Grove of the Ancients, wherein reside members of the Society of Alms, the young Keltan could see how one could be attracted to this life of adventure.

As the sun was going down on their sixth day out of Mangohal, the group heard noises from somewhere further up the dirt-strewn path. Without a word, Grim flexed his powerful wings and took flight in that direction. He was no more than thirty wing strokes away when his spell of Concealment activated and he slipped from Ferika's view. However, from the way Cavazos continued to track his eyes across the sky, she figured he was able to pierce through the magic of his friend's spell.

Ivara began to stretch the road weariness out of her muscles as Cavazos untethered Tempest and began to dismount. He caught Ferika's eye and motioned for her to remain on horseback. Seeing the youth reach for her fighting sticks, the gnome shook his head and instead gestured towards the bow. The gnome disappeared into the thickening woods, using the shadows to remain hidden from the casual eye. Ivara nudged her horse into a slow walk up the path towards what became apparent as sounds of battle. The other horses followed her lead, and Ferika used that time to string her bow and ensure that the arrows would slide easily from the quiver.

"By Bran's bushy beard, I'll have your head for that!" boomed the voice of Grim as he appeared to enter the fray.

"Arrows out, but remain on horseback if you are able," whispered Ivara as she slid from her mount and tied her and Grim's horse to a nearby tree. She then hurried towards the sound of battle easily outpacing Ferika's horse that was only then beginning a fast trot. Since Grim did not come back from his reconnaissance mission, Feri figured the situation was most dire.

What she found less than five minutes later was a scene of utter chaos. Three wagons were strewn haphazardly across the ground. One of them was on fire and Ferika could make out the charred limbs of at least two children that were not able to escape the inferno. A large orceen female was doing her best to extricate another screaming child from the conflagration while also fending off the attacks of two warriors dressed in dark-gray armor, with an orange sash adorned with strange hieroglyphics around their waist.

A second wagon lay no more than fifteen feet from the first. A few small boxes, bedrolls, and other equipment used during travel were scattered all around. Two men stood side by side, fending off the advance of several warriors, and their two-headed hound.

The third wagon had been flipped completely upside down and had landed on the legs of a man, who was even then trying desperately to extricate himself. A young boy was pulling at the man, perhaps doing more harm than good, even as an older looking girl was rushing to their aid. An arrow, burst from the growing gloom to pierce the calf of the girl who cried out in pain and stumbled to the ground.

Without thinking, Feri tracked the path of the arrow and sent one of her own in that direction. She did not know if she hit her target and really didn't care since there were three of the orange-sashed warriors engaged in combat with Ivara and two more headed towards the young Keltan. Feri hauled on the reins, getting her horse to cut left across the scene, putting a few trees between herself and the warriors. She worked her bow furiously and sent several arrows their way. She was sure one hit, but could not tell if any of the others had scored. Just as she was turning to scan for more targets, an arrow whizzed within an inch of her face. She glanced up in time to see the enemy archer let fly with another arrow. However, the arrow went widely astray as the archer's knee exploded with a sound of thunder as Cavazos made his introduction into the fray.

Ferika continued on her arc around the killing field, picking her shots. She saw that Grim was surrounded by the corpses of four of the warriors and was locked in a tense back and forth battle with a large orceen, whose large tusks and porcine face spoke more to his orcish bloodline than to that of his human parent. While the Keltan sorely wanted to help her friend, she feared she was just as likely to harm Grim as she was to hit his foe. She would have to trust in the dwarf's skill and see where she would be of better use.

The Keltan had just sent an arrow into the left butt cheek of a tall female, when she noticed an orthos slip past the guard of one a wagon defenders and chomp down on the unfortunate's neck. The beast resembled a two headed dog, with alligator-like scales, sharp claws and a long powerful tail. Ferika had not seen an orthos before, but had heard they could stand as tall as six feet at the shoulders. She estimated this must be a young specimen as it was not that tall, but had heard enough about these unterland dwellers to understand the man's life was forfeit. She shot an arrow only to have it bounce uselessly off the creature's scaly hide. She quickly intoned a pray to Danu, drawing magic into the arrow that increased its sharpness and density. This time, her arrow pierced one of the creature's necks, but also continued into the chest of its victim. Ferika took small comfort in knowing the man would have died anyway, and was thankful she had not tried to help Grim in the same manner.

She was just raising her bow to loose another arrow at the orthos when Ivara grabbed the beast by the tail, flexed her muscles and flung it up against the burning wagon. She then bared her fangs, extended her claws, and rushed the recovering hound. Her attack was more fury then finesse as she and the orthos came together in a ball of teeth, claws, and scales.

A blast of lighting came from somewhere to her left, and Ferika turned in time to see Cavazos interpose himself between the two children struggling to liberate their trapped father and a trio of warriors. One of the men fell dead, with a lighting-fueled hole in his chest. The other two spread out, and approached Cavazos more cautiously. But even before they could attack, one of them went down as a heavyset man jumped on his back and bore him down to the ground. The man, dressed in farmer's garb, bashed the warriors head into the ground repeatedly and did not stop even after blood began to poor from his victim's skull.

Seeing the fate of his comrade, the third warrior turned to flee, only to stop as an arrow bloomed in his chest.

Though Ferika was aiming for his arm, she did not lament the man's passing as much as she thought she should. She quickly put him out of her mind as she continued to help in the fight wherever she saw an opening. Before long, the tide of battle shifted and the five remaining warriors fled into the woods.

Ivara dropped the broken body of the orthos to the ground and easily lifted the wagon off of the man's crushed legs. Grim and Cavazos were also helping others as Ferika rushed in to offer aid. She used healing magic on some of the more critically injured people, including the man who had been trapped. His face flushed with gratitude as the bones swiftly knit back together and the various wounds closed.

They learned that the grateful survivors (three men, six women and five children) were fleeing the village of Blustrvn, which a two-day's ride from here. The village had been sacked by the soldiers of the sash, who were part of a growing army called the Dagba Warriors. The small caravan had managed to evade detection until they ran into yet another patrol. In total, they lost nine people, as a few of the men chose to make a stand several miles back to give the others a chance to escape. Those brave souls were believed dead. If not, then they knew to meet up with the others at Mangohal.

"I am sorry we arrived so late to the scene," said Grim as he finished repairs on the single usable wagon. He then assisted Ivara and the villagers as they placed their dead gingerly within its confines.

"Ay," agreed Dacemy, the primary speaker for the group. "I am sure your blades would have saved more than a life or two, but you arrived when you did and we are glad of it."

"Well, at least you'll have some fresh horses to help

speed your travel," spoke Cavazos with a gesture towards the eleven horses they had found tied nearby. After assisting with the wounded, he and Ferika had done a check of the perimeter and of the bodies of the Dagba Warriors. They looted several of the bodies, claimed one horse for themselves, and secured a couple of valuable items from the saddlebags of the horses. The rest of the swag they left for the survivors, who took what they needed from the bodies and gladly accepted ownership of the many horses. As they had just lost everything, the swag would help provide for them over the next few tendays until they were able to figure out what to do next.

"Right you are on that score," answered Dacemy, checking to ensure the last of the bodies was properly tied down. Cavazos assumed she must have had some military training by the way she took charge of the villagers as they prepared to set out. She instructed one female adult to steer the wagon and had her flanked by two of the older children who held their newly acquired bows with at least a passing familiarity.

The other two children rode double with two adult females whose horses were positioned just ahead of the wagon. The remaining adults where mounted and positioned in a protective shell around the wagon, to which the other horses were tethered.

"May the Luck bless your trail," Dacemy said as she and the others gripped their weapons, some new, some old, and began the long journey towards Mangohal.

"And to you as well," responded Cavazos who was eying the rough map in his hands. Hearing of their journey towards the town of Tatoras, Dacemy had suggested an alternate route. It was risky as it would take them into unterland tunnels, but it would shave at least a tenday off their journey and would help them avoid the many patrols of Dagba Warriors that were determined to bring the entire region to heel.

Chapter 10:
Desire Renewed

The sturdy warrior grunted from the weight of the hammer blow he'd just blocked. Still, the force of the strike sent vibrations through his shield and tingles up the man's left arm, causing the muscles to spasm in a slight trimmer. *That's probably not a good thing*, Zendrick Retsmon thought as he gathered his wits in time to counter the axe thrust of a charging female, by expertly turning and lifting her to sail into his hammer wielding foe. Zendrick wasted no time gauging the effect of his tactic as she sheer instinct caused him to take a half step to the left and turn his right shoulder in time to avoid a spear thrust from yet another combatant.

"By Khakaba's crusty codpiece, I really liked that shawl," Zendrick lamented as the head of the spear punched a hole in the intricately designed, fleece-lined, pullover that hung from his broad shoulders. As if conjuring strength from the very mention of the God of Storms, Zendrick unleashed a downpour of attacks at the spear wielder, that had the outclassed warrior backpedaling and turning until he bumped up against the woman and hammer-wielding warrior who were only then once again gaining their proper balance.

The warlord rushed the three warriors, easily sidestepping the attacks of the smaller foes as his concentration was centered primarily on the hammer wielding behemoth with a green eye patch, more muscle than brains, and a glint in his eyes that whispered that he had just a cat's whisker's length shy of insane. *You sure do know how to pick em*, the Zendrick thought as he sent out a vicious left jab, using the edge of his round shield as a cudgel against the man's exposed throat. As the man dropped his hammer, instinctively raising his hands to his crushed throat, Zendrick leapt up to punch his right knee into the warrior's abdomen.

The impact of the female's axe landed hard on Zendrick's right shoulder, and he barely lifted his shield in time to deflect the tip of the spear and send it up and to the left. Even then, the weapon scored a shallow cut along his cheek and distracted him long enough for the attacker to drop the weapon and follow up with a heavy punch of his own.

Zendrick accepted the punch as a lesson not to rest on past successes. His many years of combat training, and actual battle experience, allowed him to take some of the bite out of the punch as he allowed his body to flow with the strike, turning his body and dropping down low to sweep the man's legs from under him. Quick as a cat, Zendrick bashed the pummel of his axe twice into the man's face, knocking him unconscious, before standing to face the rapidly approaching female, and the warriors still in her wake.

Though the lovely brown skinned female was not as physically imposing as Zendrick, she struck boldly and without hesitation. The speed and accuracy of her strikes had the warlord at a momentary disadvantage until he began to recognize her overreliance on the Ostervin Fighting Style, favored by many pit fighters from the Outlands. The style was built to deliver quick and decisive victory. It relied on economical strikes intended to deliver maximum harm. However, Ostervin Niatnudis (the riven who invented the fighting technique) did not place much value in a strong defense and so the style often left its user open to counter attacks from skilled foes. And so, when the fierce female reacted too aggressively to one of his feints, leaving her left side exposed, Zendrick was quick to send his axe in and open a deep wound that showered the battleground with bright red blood and took yet another foe out of commission.

And then there were four, Zendrick thought as he ducked low to avoid the sword of another attacker, then quickly shifted his stance to send the flat of his axe streaking towards the abdomen of the next warrior in line, scoring a hit that knocked the exhausted soldier to the ground where he wisely stayed, hungrily sucking in great gulps of air. Seeing his comrade fall, the first warrior's steps faltered for a split second, but it was all the distraction Zendrick needed to bring his right foot up and deliver a solid blow to the warrior's head sending the unconscious man flying into a nearby pile of hay. Allowing the momentum of the kick to turn him completely, the aging warrior was well positioned to face the two remaining fighters as they advanced on him in measured steps.

A line of blood trickled down from a cut under Zendrick's right eye and his left arm stung where a blow had landed above the guard of his shield. A grim look of determination crossed his face as he rushed the two men, bashing his shield into one, while using his axe to deflect a sword blow from the other. The two men were seasoned warriors that had fought many battles together and thus their attacks were well coordinated. The trio soon found themselves in a deadly dance of strike, block, counter-strike, block, feint, and repeat. Long minutes went by, and though each side had scored hits on the other, none seemed to be able to gain a decisive advantage. Zendrick's thoughts drifted to the pendant on his chest, and he surmised that if he tapped into its might, he could turn the tide against these two, but he refused to do so.

Instead, he stepped back from his foes, dropped his axe and shield and said, "Halt. Though I am sure you to were not trying your level best, I was still not able to overcome you. It appears I still have much to learn."

"While you clearly did not win, you did manage to give me another beauty mark," said Snuzrig, a seven-foot tall orceen with greenish-gray skin and large tusks, evincing more of his mother's orc heritage than that of his human father, as he wiped his bloody arm with a filthy rag lying nearby.

"That's just because you're getting sloppy, and kept dropping your left arm too low," chided Rolinger dryly. Zendrick and Snuzrig both looked askance at the handsome beardless gnome whose black hair was braided in long cornrows down his scalp. Standing nearly three feet tall, Rolinger might be mistaken for a human child where it not for his deeply muscled physique, confident swagger, and red skin that glowed in the torchlight of the open-air training hall.

"In truth, my lord, you should have lost your life four times tonight, were this not a training exercise. Your skills have vastly improved since we first met four years ago, but you still overestimate your *strength* relative to your opponent's *skill*," the gnome finished before dawning his armor.

"It is hard for me to deny the truth of your words, seeing as how you are the only one in this place without a scratch on them even though you forsook to protection of armor," replied Zendrick while moving to check the other warriors in the hall. The soldiers on the field were all battle tested and so most were tending to their own wounds. Mortrig, a large human with stringy red hair and a wide frame, was bending over and examining Urtrak, who remained unconscious.

Though Zendrick was concerned that the smaller Urtrak had not yet recovered from his blow, a spike of pride bloomed in his chest as he noted the dented helmet and the swollen skin around it that had brought the experienced warrior down. "Mortrig, go see if Vellubus is still awake and ask him to come provide aid. If not, then carry Urtrak to the medic building to be tended by one of Vellubus' underlings."

"I will do as you say, my lord," answered Mortrig before leaving.

"Walk with me," Zendrick said to the two remaining men as he gathered his weapons and strolled down the length of the training hall. His boots made soft shuffling sounds as they passed over the sand dusted wood. The long rectangular room of wood and brick construction contained several weapon's racks, various stacks of hay simulating obstacles that might be found on a battlefield, and had enough space to host up to fifty warriors at once.

Outside, the night sky was clear and both of Mythandria's moons could clearly be seen. Zendrick pulled his heavy cowl a bit tighter against the chill coming off the ocean as the trio crested a sand dune and looked out over the crashing waves. In the distance, Zendrick could just make out the silhouette of Demarnia. As always, he was more than a little happy to be away from that island.

"I'm in no rush to be stepping foot upon that cursed isle any time soon," spoke Snuzrig.

"Aye," agreed Rolinger as he ran his hands through the tall swaying grass and exhilarated at the biting touch of ocean mist. Even as the gnome allowed his body to relax, his eyes constantly scanned the area for any threats to his lord. After years of working with Snuzrig, he knew the orceen was doing the same.

Turning his gaze from the water, Zendrick looked down upon his new stronghold that was nearing completion. The fortifications were solid, with heavy walls surrounding nine inner buildings, a small but fertile garden, and an underground well that provided the fort's fresh water. Work was still being done on a host of buildings outside of the fortress where a quarter of Zendrick's growing army would be housed. The rest of his forces were spread out in smaller villages within easy reach should they be called into action. True, this place was not nearly as impressive as the citadel Solas had constructed on Demarnia, but Zendrick never felt at ease when on the island and so he had made the decision to relocate his base of operations to this spot. At first, Solas and his masters of the Brood had objected, but they understood it was the best way to keep Zendrick in line and allowed the warlord to proceed with his plan. Ultimately, Solas seemed to agree it was a good decision and had not mentioned the matter in several years.

"Work is progressing well, I see," uttered words that sent an instant shiver of resignation down Zendrick's spine, and their speaker appeared as if conjured out of the very night itself.

"Yes," answered Zendrick, whose strong voice hid well the disquiet in his heart. Over the years, he had come to understand more about the nature of the one standing before him. So he was not surprised to find his two most trusted bodyguards fast asleep on the ground, likely victim of a spell from Solas.

"Was that strictly necessary?" asked the warlord as he gestured to the helpless warriors.

"Truthfully, no," the darkling responded, allowing a bit of mirth into his words. "But just as you test your strength, so too must I always hone my abilities. That chroas gnome of yours has proven to be quite resistant to all manner of spells. I had thought to speak with you this night and simply could not pass up the opportunity that presented itself."

"Well, I'm sure he won't be as jovial about it as you are," responded the human as he turned to give the approaching figure his full attention. As usual, Solas was dressed in a long black robe that flowed around him, seemingly consuming his slight frame. Since the sun had set many hours ago, the darkling did not have the cowl of his garment pulled up and Zendrick stared into Solas' eyes, for only there could he see the spark of life hidden beneath the dead husk the thing wore. Solas wheezed out a hollow cough as something akin to a ridged tentacle wiggled its way across his face, momentarily misshaping the overly taught pale skin.

"So, have you come to tutor me more in matters of the arcane, or has Master Nimrotha sent you to me on a more urgent mission?" inquired Zendrick, getting straight to the point.

"Other matters are afoot that must be addressed. And so, no, I am not here on personal matters," replied Solas, eyeing his pupil appraisingly as he considered the many changes that had evolved in their relationship.

Where at first Zendrick was simply a useful pawn, easily manipulated due to his foolish lust for power, the years since the loss of the child at Silverwood had taught the human patience and a proper understanding of his place in the world. The warlord wisely chose to bend the knee to Nimrotha, a member of the Brood, once he became aware of the broader schemes at play in the game in which he had unwittingly become a player. It was only then that Solas developed his first inkling of respect for the human, and why he agreed to begin instructing Zendrick in the arena of spellcasting and the understanding of occult knowledge.

But the changes had not stopped there. Zendrick had sought to grow stronger of his own accord, without overmuch reliance on spells and enchanted items. To that end, he had begun to train with warriors of true skill, forsaking his past paths of victory that relied on sheer strength and savagery. The warlord became a more respected leader as he became more active on the field of battle and began to utilize strategies that resulted in more victories than wins. The size of Zendrick's force had more than tripled over the years and this was in no small part because he had a reputation of being someone that the needs of his warriors, and most of their desires, which often ranged from the illicit to the downright depraved, were taken care of.

"The time has come to retrieve the child," Solus uttered into the empty night.

Those words smashing against Zendrick's mind like the waves battering the nearby shores. The warlord's hand clenched the pummel of his axe as he recalled the day he had lost the child, and his temper. Like a petulant child he'd had every man, woman, and child in the village put to death and ordered the entire area burned to cinders. At the time, he was elated to hear the cries of his victims, but now... Now seldom did a night go by that he wasn't plagued by the plaintiff wails of those that needlessly suffered due to his impetuous actions. It wasn't that Zendrick had an issue with killing, far from it. No, he was quite used to killing. But on that long ago day his warriors had devolved into animals that satiated their savage pleasures against the villagers, and the worst part is, he had done so too.

"Why now? And why do they need her still? I thought the alignment had passed and it was no longer possible to siphon her power and use it in the manner previously intended," Zendrick snorted, allowing a bit of defiance, *but not anger*, to sound in the timber of his voice. In truth, he still was not sure exactly what the Brood had wanted the child for, but he knew it was not to enhance the pendant and give him more power, which was the lie Solas had originally sold to him.

"It has been thirteen years since you lost the child, and in the time you have grown old. But I see that is not a bad thing. Yes, your hair is grayer and your skin has more scars, but your body has become harder and your mind sharper," Solas whispered as he stepped forward and gripped Zendrick's arms with hands that were cold as the grave, forcing an involuntary gasp from Zendrick. The darkling's dead eyes flickered with an inner fire as he stared into the warlord's brown orbs. "Take a stab at it, bright boy. Answer your own question, old man."

The pair stood in silence for some minutes as Zendrick's mind crawled through a myriad of possible answers. He contemplated everything he had learned of the Brood, three beings of strange power and origin that were believed to be half-infernal creatures possessed of near immortality. He then looked up to consider the comet and its red tail that blazed in the night's sky. "Though the initial ritual called for the death of a newborn, they have likely discovered some other rite to be carried out under the Blood Moon that will accomplish much of the same. The Child of Dream's access to the old magic appears to be the key they need to open the door of ascension they so desperately crave."

Solas released the warlord and turned once again to face the ocean. "Well done, bright boy. Your answer is more right than wrong. The Brood is nothing if not patience, and there is indeed significance in the advent of the Blood Moon. Yet, that is not the only reason why we are only now moving to retrieve the child. While the Brood has always known where the child was being kept, there were circumstance that precluded them from taking action. However, conditions have changed and the time to avenge an old betrayal is at hand."

The darkling's form began to take on a transparent quality as he slowly ascended on the wind. "You are to muster half your force within the tenday. Prepare supplies for a six-month campaign, though this matter should be resolved well before that. When all is prepared, I and some of my fellow darklings will return to accompany you. You will give the orders to your men, but the operation will be led by Winchunset Na'Fallow."

A thousand thoughts cluttered Zendrick's mind, but none beat out the dread that filled him over the thought of traveling with the Handmaiden of Serafeen. The stunned warlord moved to voice his displeasure only to realize that the darkling had receded with the wind, leaving the warrior on unstable shores.

"I can't say that sounds promising," Rolinger stated, as the gnome moved through the tall grass to stand by his lord's side.

Zendrick, who was only partially surprised to find

that Solas' spell had not worked on the dangerous gnome, took comfort in the knowledge that there were matters of which even the Brood appeared ignorant. "I take it you heard everything?" he inquired.

"Exactly so, and while this news does not come without significant peril, it may offer the exact opportunity we have been waiting for," answered the gnome whose lips creased with the beginnings of a grin.

Chapter 11:
Changing Tides

Lorat fidgeted in his seat, and wondered to himself for the third time in less than fifteen minutes, why the chairs in this place were so blasted uncomfortable. Surely, Knikwing Perin could afford to get some of the plush toosh fluffers that adorned the chairs of many of the finer establishments in Sunder's Dawn. The draken owner of Perin's Pike, the establishment he had been ordered to wait in, must have been raking in silver by the handfuls, since the tavern was always filled. Given that this was the only place in the whole hamlet where members of the various gangs could come for fun and entertainment, without worrying about getting a dagger in the back the patrons were likely to stay longer, and spend more liberally than they would at other establishments.

Knikwing Perin had come to Sunder's Dawn a few years back. The half-brawn half-fire dragon was flush with silver and bought a few run-down buildings in the seedier parts of the hamlet. Sparing no expense, he hired skilled artisans and craftsmen to breathe new life into the decrepit structures. One, he turned into a magnificent villa, with an expansive courtyard complete with a pool covered by glass walls commonly reserved for green houses. The few people Lorat knew that had been within the structure said no matter what season it was, the temperature within the structure was always warm and humid. Lorat a suspected there was magic afoot in that construction, but couldn't say for sure.

Two of Knikwing's other buildings had been renovated. They looked beautiful on the outside, but Lorat had never heard of anyone that had ever been within one of them, since even the contractors that worked on the buildings had disappeared. If anyone within Sunder's Dawn knew what business went on within those walls, their ability to keep the secret would be enough to impress even Volarin, the God of Shadows.

Prior to opening the doors to his three-story tavern, Knikwing arranged a meeting with the heads of all the gangs of Sunder's Dawn. Lorat had heard the meeting started out quite contentiously, but somehow Knikwing was able to convince, coerce, or bribe the leaders to decree Perin's Pike would be a violence-free zone. Since the tavern's grand opening, to this very day, that decree had only been broken twice, and both times the offenders disappeared only for their mangled corpses to turn up in public places days later. No one could ever say definitively what happened to them, but all got the message, and the truce within the Pike's walls is nigh inviolate.

Lorat opened the scrunched-up parchment laying on the table before him, and read the words once again.

Lorat,
It is ordained that you meet us at Perin's Pike. The time of our arrival shall be two hours past the sun's zenith, three days hence. Do not make us wait or have to come find you.

- He Who Is They

His fingers shook as he nervously glanced around and began trying to press the wrinkles out of the parchment. The letter had been waiting in his room when he woke up three days ago. After reading it, he had balled it up and thrown it on the ground, promising not be cowed by his uncle. But that false bravado lasted only a few breaths before he scooped the parchment up and read the missive once more. It had been three very long days full of doubt and worry, and as the young man sat staring at the door, he prayed that he had gotten the gist of the letter and that he had not missed meeting his uncle. It had been a full three hours past noon and still no sign of Losaginus X (or as he had started calling himself, He Who is They).

Lorat's mind was just forming the start of a poetic stream of curses concerning the lamentable quality of Perin's inadequate buttock preservers, when the door opened and two azure clad figure stepped in. "Here he comes," the suddenly terrified Lorat thought as a stout man with dusky skin, a bald head, and midnight-black eyes walked in their wake.

Lorat ran a hand nervously through his hair, and tried his best to compose himself as he watched the purplish-black shadows bleed off the man's skin. "Uh, w… welcome uncle," stammered the young man as he scrambled to his feet and pulled out the seat on the opposite side of the table.

Without saying a word, one of the blue-clad figures stalked directly at Lorat, and did not stop until the retreating man bumped into the chair he had just left.

"Sit," came a female voice, from within the darkness of the cloak's cowl.

"Sure, I was just…" began Lorat, vaguely aware that many of the tavern's patrons were watching the exchange closely.

"Don't speak," was all the figure said, the young man deflated into his chair. Only then, did the cloaked servant step two paces back, allowing Lorat to watch as his uncle took a seat in the opposite chair. Lorat swallowed the bile rising in his throat as terror exploded within his heart.

Lorat had standing within the X Town Growlers because he was the leader's nephew. But Losaginus X had only agreed to look after the boy out of an obligation to Lorat's mother. Losaginus X had moved them from Kriasta when he learned of his sister's lingering illness. He dearly loved Miszrilla, but thought her son was lazy and uninspired. Still, he had Lorat initiated into the gang and ordered his men to look after the youth.

However, Lorat had not seen his uncle once in the last two years since her passing. He had heard rumors of his uncle's increasingly sadistic behavior and that he had begun referring to himself as He Who Is They. Those thoughts and more flitted through his mind as Lorat could barely recognize his uncle in the man that now sat across from him. Black eyes had replaced those of light brown hue and gray-black skin covered a frame that was once pale white. But most disturbing were the shadows that flowed off the man's skin as dust disturbed by a gentle breeze.

"We had suspected all along that you were unfit for

this... or any life," began He Who Is They with words that sounded as if uttered by multiple voices at once. "This one's sister managed to convince us otherwise, and for a time it looked as if you might become worthy. But that potential faded with Miszrilla's passing. Since that time, you have been not but disappointment made flesh. You have leveraged your kinship with us to garner some semblance of obeisance amongst the lower ranks of our organization, but used it to fulfil your base desires and have not but utter waste to show for it."

Lorat, thought briefly that he should make a dash for the door, but knew his trembling legs would prove too cowardly to perform such a task. Instead, he found his head unconsciously nodding a confirmation as fear drowned out the words that continued to tumble from his uncle's mouth.

"...and now we catch word of your latest failure. We hear the laughter of these mewling peasants as they croon about how the X Town Growlers were brought low by three nobodies. Our ranks are depleted, though only slightly, by the loss of those sent to rectify your current shortcomings. Other gangs had thought to exploit our perceived weakness. Though they have been taught the folly of their ways, you have wrought shame upon the organization. Shame upon us. And all for a little piece of skrim, which you could have easily had in any one of our flophouses."

"But, I..." Lorat started, thinking to defend his actions.

"We do not want to hear your words," He Who Is They hissed. "Many called for your death for they only tolerated your existence due to our presence. But in our wisdom, we have decided your flesh could be put to a better use. You will come with us, and we will make of you a useful tool."

With that, He Who Is They stood and walked towards the door. Realizing that whatever his uncle had in store for him might be worse than death, Lorat's traitorous body finally responded to his desperate command and he leapt out of his chair. He dashed across the room, weaving his way past tables and patrons alike, allowing a small smile to crease his lips as he burst through the Pike's door and tasted the sunlight on his skin. Just then, all went black as a mace bashed into the side of his skull sending his blood and consciousness into the ether.

"Ever the fool," whispered He Who Is They as his words squirmed their way into Lorat's brain, bringing the young man fully awake.

Lorat found himself laying on his back, with his naked body shackled to a cold stone slab. Swiveling his head, he could make out vague shapes in what appeared to be a dungeon. The air was moist and stank of mildew. Drops of liquid drew the young man's eyes towards the stone ceiling and the figure that appeared out of the gloom. The terror within him, matched the terror he saw in the eyes of the naked shakaran who was magically suspended five feet above him. Deep runes had been carved into the feline humanoid's body, from which blood dripped.

Chanting sounded somewhere to Lorat's left, but try as he might, the youth could not crane his head far enough to see the chanter. That wouldn't have mattered anyway, since his attention was instantly captured by the anguish that erupted from the shakaran. Glowing lines slowly began to appear on the fur covered hide of the shakaran, and Lorat found himself screaming out in desperation as he realized that the light was forming as something on the inside of the shakaran was attempting to clawing its way out.

As the chanting grew in intensity, so too did the light, which spilled as a jagged rift opened across the torso of the shakaran, whose hoarse screams lingered in Lorat's mind even as the shakaran's life slipped away.

Lorat never had much aptitude for spellcasting, but had heard of blood rituals that could provide access to the various planes of the realm. Gazing at the vast space contained within the corpse, his mind fought hard to make sense of what he was seeing. A lightning rich storm rolled across an endless expanse of orange and brown, as wormlike forms of various sizes undulated within the thick morass. To his dismay, the worm-things were drawing closer, tearing at each other in an attempt to be the first to breach the corpse and find purchase in Mythandria.

Lorat struggled to free himself, ignoring the pain on his wrist and ankles as the shackles tore into his flesh. But in the end, he could only watch as a black wormlike creature, easily ten feet long and half a foot wide, squirmed its way out of a mass of red, orange, yellow and white shapes to slip free of the shakaran's corpse and fall ponderously upon Lorat's quivering form.

Tears streamed from Lorat's bulging eyes, but no sound escaped his anguished body as the worm-thing slithered its way down his throat, filling him completely. Pain of unbelievable magnitude lanced the youth's mind as the creature supplanted his organs and very tissues with its fowl taint. The aethereal nature of the alien being enabled massive bulk to adapt to the confines of the human frame, and it relished the feel of flesh and blood.

"Your time is at an end," came an internal voice that Lorat heard within the increasingly small sliver of awareness he still occupied. "Fear not, for you exist within us and are now one with the Slythryn."

Five days later, Lorat sat in the well-appointed dining room of He Who Is They and sucked the blood and viscera off his dusky fingers. He had just finished consuming the last of the five warriors that had been bound and brought before him. The skills and knowledge of the five people were now his and he sat with his eyes closed as his body acclimated to the new input.

The creature that called itself Lorat knew he was more than the pathetic human who had wasted so much potential in the times before the joining. Their once frail body had been enhanced by the infusion of the slythryn, a race of beings that existed in the space between the planes. In their native home, slythryns exist as a massive hive mind with hierarchies broken down by hue, with black-hued slythryns occupying the top of the pyramid.

Having been loosed into the world, Lorat shared a telepathic link with the seven other slythryns that were given new life by the leader of the X Town Growlers. Unlike He Who Is They, who still shared consciousness with Losaginus X, the minds of the other slythryn hosts proved to be far more pliable and were quickly supplanted by the invading intelligence.

Deep shadows swirled to life as Lorat stood and walked from the room. The parasitic slythryn was still acclimating to its new form, and thus Lorat's movements were a bit awkward. He Who Is They had prepared him for this and explained he would have full mastery of the body's potential within a tenday. But he could sense the desire of the other offspring to please their progenitor, and so Lorat was determined to begin the hunt.

Stepping out into the hallway, Lorat nodded at the waiting slythryn who lowered their heads deferentially. As he proceeded down the hallway, four azure-clad slythryns walked in his wake and would accompany him on his quest. The quintet walked through the double doors at the end of the hallway where they all bowed low to their sire, He Who Is They.

"Ah, we are pleased to see you have at last come into the fullness of life," He Who Is They said, as he beckoned Lorat closer so he might better inspect his progeny. Lorat was aware that verbal communication was not necessary amongst their kind, but He Who Is They insisted they communicate in this manner to continue to hone their control of all of their host's abilities. Satisfied, He Who Is They stepped aside and presented Lorat with a midnight gray suit of leather armor, a dazzling sword and a wondrously crafted razor whip. The parasite within Lorat could smell the magic coming off of the items and luxuriated in the feel as he donned them.

"This is Orpsol. She will guide your hunt for the three who brought shame into our life. We would prefer to have them brought to us alive, but will accept having their heads as offering, if the former possibility eludes you," He Who Is They said, drawing Lorat's gaze to the green-clad female standing several feet away. As host to a green slythryn, Orpsol was a master at tracking and would locate their prey no matter where the path led.

"Your will, is our destiny," the six offspring proclaimed in unison before heading to their sire's stable and the infernal steeds that had been prepared for them.

As the Frozen Moon cast her glance upon the land, six specters of darkness departed the gates of Sunder's Dawn on a mission of death.

To be continued in

CHILD OF LOSS

DREAM WAR SAGA, VOL. 2.

Story by David Thompson
Based on the Realm of EverLore

About the Author

David Thompson is a husband, father, and educator living in Cincinnati, Ohio. He is the creator of the tabletop roleplaying game, EverLore. The inspiration for the game springs from his dreams. The passion to reach his goals comes from the desire to craft a world of diversity where all people can find positive representation and imagine the hope of a brighter future.

His sons grew up listening to him talking about the game and how it would be complete *"one day."* They watched as he spent endless hours researching past cultures, improving his drawing skills, and discussing one aspect or another of the world with just about anyone who would listen. Even on days when the task seemed too hard and Dave doubted it was possible, they always believed. Eventually, the fantasy bug bit them as well and for several years they too have been adding their insights to deepen the lore of the realm.

Child of Dreams is the first novel of EverLore to cross the threshold from dream to reality, but it will not be the last. Dave will continue working on his tabletop game and novels for EverLore, and plans to *"one day"* produce video games and live action movies.

He hopes you enjoyed this novel, and invites you to join him on this journey of imagination and wonder.

Experience the Expansive Realm of EverLore

Continue the adventure with the EverLore roleplaying game. Our core books are:

- **Traveler's Compendium**
- **Monsters Menagerie (for Lore Masters)**
- **Chronicler's Delight (for Lore Masters)**

Witness the birth of Mythandria and gain insight on its cultures and factions by reading our Lore books:

- **Inception, Origins of Mythandria**
- **Thy Kindgoms Come (for Lore Masters)**

Explore our website for products, hours of videos, free downloads, and more.

Support ManChild, Ltd. by purchasing your copy of EverLore, becoming a member on our site, or subscribing to our Twitch channels. You can also follow us on social media ***@EverLoreGame***.

www.ManChildLtd.com

www.Twitch.Tv/EverLoreGame

www.Twitch.Tv/EssenceOfEverLore

BOUNDLESS

Let the Adventure Begin!

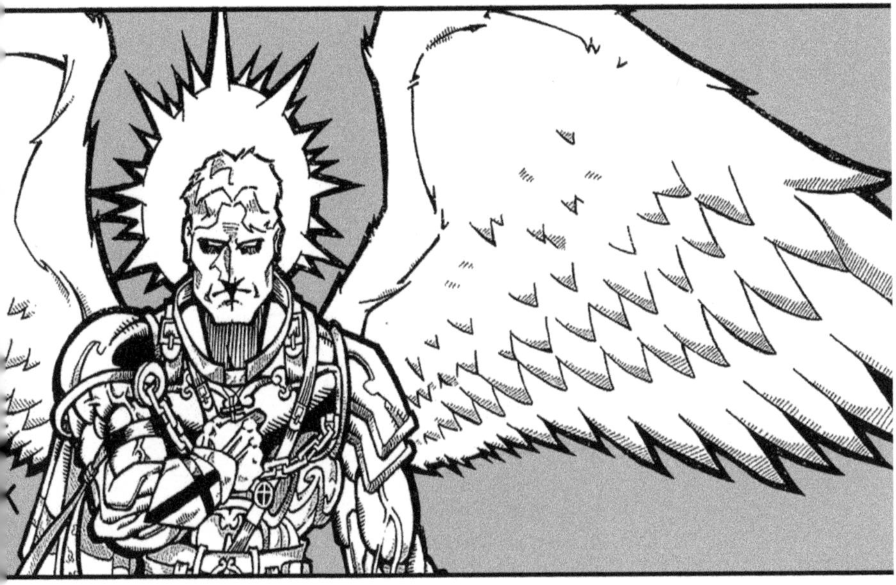

EverLore is a roleplaying game with lots of diversity and inclusion that is not limited by classes or levels.

Lore Masters can familiarize themselves with our system while shepherding a party through the Golden City Saga. This eight-module campaign is comprised of the following titles:

- Sword of Justice
- Craven Cor
- Damsel's Fate
- Rouge Justice
- Turbulent Seas
- Shadows of Ajulon
- La Desprata
- The Golden City

This Game is for You!
ManChildLtd.com

BoundLess

@EverLoreGame

www.ingramcontent.com/pod-product-compliance
Ingram Content Group UK Ltd.
Pitfield, Milton Keynes, MK11 3LW, UK
UKHW020224250726
13967UKWH00001B/184

9 781951 259181